CLEAVER
OF THE
GOOD LUCK
DINER

CLEAVER
OF THE
GOOD LUCK
DINER

JAMES DUFFY

CHARLES SCRIBNER'S SONS • NEW YORK

Charles Scribner's Sons Books for Young Readers
Macmillan Publishing Company
866 Third Avenue, New York, NY 10022
Collier Macmillan Canada, Inc.

Printed in the United States of America
First Edition   10 9 8 7 6 5 4 3 2 1

Library of Congress Cataloging-in-Publication Data
Duffy, James, date
Cleaver of the Good Luck Diner/James Duffy.—1st ed.
p.   cm.
Summary: Clever Cleaver, the big dog at the Good Luck Diner, keeps things stirred up for the family that runs the diner and works at effecting a reconciliation between the estranged parents.
[1. Dogs—Fiction. 2. Restaurants, lunchrooms, etc.—Fiction. 3. Family life—Fiction.] I. Title.
PZ7.D87814Cl   1989   ISBN 0–684–18969–0
[Fic]—dc19   88–29906   CIP   AC

For the one and only
AWA PALOMA MUGATARI

CLEAVER
OF THE
GOOD LUCK
DINER

1

"Cleaver wants his ice cream, Mom," Cori yelled.

"He can't have it today. He's getting fat," Mom yelled back from the kitchen.

"You can't have any today," Cori told Cleaver. "You're getting too fat."

Cleaver put his front paws up on the counter. He leaned over the counter and licked Cori in the face until she turned her stool away from him. Cleaver reached out his left paw, the one he shook hands with. He put it on Cori's shoulder and barked. He waited. Cori didn't move. He barked again, louder this time.

"Hey, Mom," Cori yelled, "Cleaver's barking for his ice cream."

"I can hear him," Mom answered. "Take him out back and tie him up."

Cleaver heard Mom. He got down from the counter

and ran to the end of the counter where the ice-cream freezer was. He lay down, wagging his tail. Cori grabbed his collar. Cleaver rolled over onto his back and wagged his tail. Cori grabbed his collar from underneath. Cleaver rolled onto his stomach. He slurped at Cori's face and wagged his tail.

"Mom," Cori yelled, "I can't get him up. He keeps rolling over. He wants his ice cream."

It was time for me to get in the middle, the way I did most afternoons when Cleaver didn't get his dish of ice cream. I went into the kitchen. Mom was making macaroni and cheese with olives and pepperoni, the Thursday-night special. It was hot in the kitchen and Mom was in a bad mood. I could see that.

"I'll give him just a little bit. Then I'll tie him up under the maple tree and come help you," I suggested.

Mom stopped slicing pepperoni to give me a hard look. "Sarah, do you really believe we have to give that dog a dish of banana ice cream every day of his life?"

"Well, he expects it now, Mom, and he won't do anything until he gets it. Anyway, he knows you promised it to him last year. You told him you'd give him ice cream every day of his life. Cleaver remembers things."

"That was when he was still a puppy. I didn't know he was going to grow up to be a grizzly bear and eat us out of house and home. Look at him out there; he's still growing. Anyway, he's an outside dog. He should stay outside."

"But you did promise, Mom. You have to keep your promises. That's what you tell Cori and me."

My mother sighed. Cleaver was a problem, no question about it. But it wasn't all his fault. Last year after Cleaver chased away the robber who tried to stick up the diner, Mom promised him a bowl of ice cream every day as a reward.

"It would have been cheaper to give the guy the money in the drawer," Mom said, the way she always did. "It was only seventeen dollars. That's not more than three weeks' worth of ice cream."

"He'll eat vanilla or strawberry instead of banana if you coax him," Cori piped up. She had come into the kitchen to listen. "But he won't eat chocolate. No way. I wonder why. Chocolate is my favorite."

"All right," Mom said, the way she always did. "Give him a sixty-cent scoop of banana—not the ninety-cent scoop, mind you. And take him down to the playing field to run around."

While Cleaver gobbled up his ice cream, I remembered the evening of the holdup last year. He was only a puppy then, sleeping on his blanket under the counter. Even as a puppy he was pretty big. He was snoozing there when this guy in a leather jacket came in and walked up to the counter. Mom came out of the kitchen to ask him what he was going to have. He put his hand in his pocket as if he had a gun and said he wanted the money from the register.

There wasn't much money. We had been robbed before and Mom kept the extra money in a pot in the kitchen. She walked down behind the counter to the register, but Cleaver had his tail out and Mom stepped on it. Cleaver gave an awful howl and jumped up. He hit his head on the shelf under the counter and knocked some plates to the floor, making a lot of noise, and the robber ran out the door.

Chief Pettigrew came and said Cleaver was a good watchdog and Mom was lucky to have him. She was feeling pretty good about saving seventeen dollars and very proud of Cleaver, too, especially when they put his picture in the weekly paper with a story about how he had chased the robber. So she gave him a big kiss and promised him ice cream every day. Later, when she wanted to forget about it, neither Cori, who always snitched a little chocolate when she scooped up Cleaver's banana ice cream, nor Cleaver would let her.

When Cleaver finished, he was ready to go to the playing field and chase his tennis ball. He never asked for seconds. He licked his bowl clean and went straight to the back door to go out. He was a good dog and we all loved him, including Mom and Granny Rubin. It was just that Mom didn't think he should have banana ice cream every day.

2

Cleaver's full name is Cleaver von Pippin Gumboodle Stuart. Each of us—Mom and Dad and Cori and I—gave him a name. They're all there on the papers Mom sent off to the kennel club to register him. Stuart is Mom's married name. She said she was thinking of changing it back to Rubin when she got around to it. Sometimes we call the dog Cleve or Pip, but most of the time he's Cleaver. He seems to like that name best.

He is a very fancy dog, a genuine Bernese mountain dog, one of the big ones that weigh over a hundred pounds. Dad said he paid over four hundred dollars for him, but not to tell Mom that; she might give Cleaver back and want the money. Cleaver is black with a white face and a white chest under his chin and a white tip at the end of his bushy black tail and white feet at the end of his brown-stockinged legs, with brown eyebrows and soft brown curls under his ears. "That's the way he should look," Dad said. "All good Bernese look like Cleaver." Dad knows a lot about dogs.

Cleaver was sort of a good-bye present from Dad to his family. He brought Cleaver in to look after the house and the diner when he moved out. Mom said Dad could never stay in one place very long and we were lucky—or unlucky, she didn't know which—he stayed with her and us girls as long as he did. Whenever she was feeling good at the end of the day, sitting on a stool with Cleaver's head in her lap, scratching his ears, she'd laugh a little to herself and tell Cleaver that, all things considered, he wasn't a bad trade.

Dad didn't go far. He didn't leave Stanhope, just us. Mom borrowed money from Granny Rubin and insisted on buying his half of the Good Luck Diner and Deli. Dad took the money and bought a Winnebago to live in and opened a launderette on the other side of town by the college. It did so well that he opened another one in the shopping mall six months later, then one more over in Madison.

I guess that made him so rich he wouldn't have to work in the diner if he came back. Anyway, he came around and told Mom he was sorry and wanted to move back in. Mom said nothing doing. She had Cleaver now. He was a lot less trouble than Dad.

When Dad first started picking us up in the Winnebago for our visiting days, Cleaver forgot who he came from and growled at Dad, which made Mom smile. After a while, he wagged his tail at Dad the way he did at everyone else who came in. Cleaver would have wagged his tail at the robber if the guy had stuck around.

When we got back from the playing field, Cleaver was tired out. He slipped in the back door when Cori held it open for him, although she wasn't supposed to, and crawled onto his blanket under the plate shelf. He had to squirm to get under there now, and a lot of him stuck out, which made it hard to walk up and down behind the counter looking after customers, but he didn't mind if we stepped on him every once in a while. He'd stick his head out from under the shelf to let you know he was all right.

On Thursday nights we were usually full from five until eight, so full that people would wait outside in their cars until there were empty stools or one of the four booths was free. Granny Rubin said Thursdays were busy because working people were getting tired of eating at home during the week but didn't want to go out to an expensive place like the Stanhope Arms in the hotel or the Gourmet Kitchen, which just opened. They went to those places on Friday or Saturday nights, which were kind of slow for us, although we always had a good number of college kids who didn't have much money.

Mom said Granny Rubin had it all wrong. People came on Thursday because of the macaroni and cheese with olives and pepperoni. Cori, who always butted in, said they came to see Cleaver the Bernese mountain dog. I said that wasn't so because Cleaver was always asleep under the counter at suppertime. Cori said that didn't matter; they knew Cleaver was there and that was good enough.

In the evenings, Linda Kowelski, Cori, and I worked in back of the counter. Linda took the orders and served the food. She was in her second year at the college, studying to be a teacher. Linda came on at noon, right after class. She did her homework in one of the booths during the afternoon when it was quiet. I carried out the dirty dishes and washed them. Cori wiped the counter and the booth tables and put on the setups when customers came in. She was in charge of the ice cream, too. Granny Rubin usually sat on the wooden stool at the register at the end of the counter. There was a PA system from the counter into the kitchen, but it never worked, so there was a lot of shouting to and from the kitchen.

When Grandpa Rubin retired from the piano factory just before it went out of business, he had this idea of starting a diner and deli in Stanhope. He found an old trolley cheap in New Haven and had it hauled up and put alongside the road at the bottom of the hill. Our house is on the side of the hill.

He advertised for someone to help him make the trolley into a diner, and my dad came along. He had just flunked out of the college for fooling around. He and Grandpa Rubin added a kitchen at one end of the trolley. They widened the trolley at the back and fixed up the inside. My grandparents called it the Good

Luck Diner and Deli. Dad stayed on to marry Nettie (that's my mom—her real name is Benedicta), and Grandpa gave him half interest in the diner as a wedding present and for all the work he had done. Dad then built an addition onto the house to make room for Cori and me.

Dad was the cook when I was born. Grandpa Rubin ran the counter and the cash register. When Grandpa died, Mom took over at the counter and Granny Rubin and I helped out sometimes. Dad got bored with the diner—and with his wife, Mom said—and moved out. Mom went into the kitchen, where she wanted to be, anyway, and got some outside help for the counter work. I think that's how it all happened.

3

Friday afternoons and Saturdays were Dad's visiting days when he wasn't busy. Usually we'd go off somewhere in the Winnebago unless it was snowing; then we'd just stay in the lot next to the launderette. We'd go to the mall in Dad's car and see a movie. Afterward we'd have a hamburger and a sundae and sleep late Saturday mornings.

He came this Friday right on time, half an hour after we got home from school. He stood at the door of the diner, where he picked us up, and shouted. "Hurry up, you guys, let's go."

"Who's that?" Mom yelled from the kitchen.

"It's Dad," Cori shouted back.

"What's he want?" Mom shouted.

"Mom wants to know what you want," Cori said to Dad.

Dad sighed. "It's visiting day, Nettie." He stuck his head in and shouted toward the kitchen. For some reason he didn't like to come into the diner. He always stood outside the door to wait for us.

"So was last Friday," Mom shouted from the kitchen. "Where were you last Friday?"

"I had to go over to Madison until late on business."

"We have a telephone, Ed—two phones, as a matter of fact, one up at the house and one right here behind the counter."

I knew this would go on forever if I didn't do something. "Come on, Dad, let's go. Get your backpack, Cori."

"I already have it, dumbbell," Cori said. "It's on my back like any idiot can see." Cori is more like Mom than I am. She doesn't take any pushing around. I guess that leaves me to be more like Dad, sort of trying to be agreeable to everybody.

Dad had left the motor running. As we started down the steps we heard Mom shouting again. I went back and stuck my head in the door.

"What is it, Mom?"

"The dog. Don't forget to take Cleaver."

"We have to take Cleaver, Dad."

We heard Dad swear under his breath. He went up the steps. This time he went straight inside. We followed along. Cleaver ran out from behind the counter. He put his front paws on Dad's shoulders. He slurped Dad in the face.

"Come on, Nettie, give me a break," Dad said in a

loud voice. "Cleaver's too big. There's not room for him in the camper."

"No dog, no girls," Mom said. She bent over the meat loaf she was making for the Friday special. Friday you could have meat loaf or broiled fish for the special, or whatever else there was on the regular menu. She stood up and came to the serving window. "You know, Ed, you should have gotten a smaller dog or a bigger van. Cleaver goes with the girls. Otherwise, he just mopes around here eating banana ice cream until they come back. I don't have time for him."

Dad crossed over to the back door, where we kept Cleaver's leash. Cleaver grabbed the end and pulled Dad to the front door and down the steps to the Winnebago. He dropped the leash and scratched at the door. Next to ice cream Cleaver liked the Winnebago best.

Cori and I piled into the front seat next to Dad. He turned the motor off and leaned forward on the steering wheel. Cleaver gave a sharp yip in back. "He wants his window open," Cori said. "Cleaver likes to smell where he's going."

"Well, he can wait," Dad said. He looked at us. "What do you guys think?" he asked. "Would you like me to come back and give up all this visiting business on Fridays and Saturdays?"

"I don't know," I said slowly. "That's kind of for you and Mom to talk over and decide."

"I like the visits," Cori piped up. "We get to go to all sorts of neat places and we get to go to the mall and stay up late. Anyway," she went on, "Mom doesn't want you back. You hurt her feelings when you left."

"Sometimes a man needs more space," Dad said. "That diner was getting smaller and smaller. I just couldn't see myself spending the rest of my days in the kitchen of the Good Luck Diner and Deli. I couldn't even stand the smell of food anymore."

"Well, maybe you and Mom could trade off every week or something," I said. I missed having Dad around all the time. I was getting a little tired of the diner, too. Other kids went home after school and had fun with their friends. I went home to work. Whatever free time Mom had she gave to Cori, it seemed.

Dad turned on the motor. "You guys might start dropping hints to your mother. I'd appreciate that."

"It won't do any good," Cori said. "Mom says, 'Once gone, long gone.' She says you should find somebody else and go off to Florida or somewhere in the Winnebago and start a new life. Do you know somebody else, Dad?"

I dug my elbow into Cori's ribs. She gave me a dirty look, but she shut up.

Dad sighed again and drove out of the parking lot. "Why don't we go over to the Cape this weekend? Maybe the bluefish are running."

4

About every two months during the year after Dad left, he took us to the Cape. These were the best visiting days we had with Dad, especially if we went all the way down to Provincetown, which is a neat place to go. We'd stop about sunset along the way at a fish-and-chips place to eat and let Cleaver out. Then we'd go to the end of the Cape, where we could smell the sea and hear the waves washing up on the beach. Saturdays Dad would take his gear down by the lighthouse. Sometimes he'd fix a rod for us, but Cori and I weren't much interested in fishing unless the fish were really running and we didn't have to wait a couple of hours for a bite. We'd rather scout the dunes and build sand castles for Cleaver to tear up.

Cleaver was interested more in fishing than sand castles. He ran back and forth when Dad had his line out, barking and snapping at the foam. Every time Dad made a cast, Cleaver charged into the breakers, which made Dad mad. He'd shout at Cleaver and threaten to put him back in the camper. He'd tell Cleaver to sit. He'd sit for about two minutes. Then he'd start all over again.

It was cold and damp when we woke up Saturday morning. Cori sat up in her bunk, groaned, and slid back under the covers. Dad and I ate our doughnuts and drank hot chocolate. We left Cori in her bunk. No one was on the beach, which pleased Dad. He liked to fish all by himself. There wasn't much surf and it looked like it might rain later on. Dad sniffed the air and nodded. It was a fine day for blues, he told me. They liked to come in close on days like this. Maybe he'd catch enough to fill the freezer in the diner if we could keep Cleaver from scaring them away.

I went back up to the Winnebago for Cleaver's leash. Cori had finished the box of doughnuts and was starting in on the cornflakes. For a kid who ate so much, she stayed as thin as a hairpin. Every time I took an extra jelly bean it seemed that I gained five pounds. Granny Rubin said Mom was fat when she was growing up. Mom said she was chunky, not fat. Dad used to tease her, asking how she could tell the difference. I wasn't even chunky, but I knew I would be if I ate like Cori. We put Cleaver on his leash and started down the beach along the high-tide line.

Sometimes we'd find all sorts of junk—broken sunglasses, a sneaker, tangled fishlines, one time a lobster trap we took home to catch raccoons in (but it didn't work), lots of cans and bottles, and driftwood. Cori would look inside all the bottles to see if there was a message from someone, but so far she hadn't found any.

It started to drizzle about noon and we headed up in the dunes to an abandoned shack we knew about. One day in the summer we found some college kids there in sleeping bags, but today it was empty. We were bored and a little disappointed with this visit. Beaches aren't much fun in the rain. Cleaver stretched out on the floor while Cori and I huddled against the wall where the roof didn't leak.

Cori put her head on her knees and looked sadly out the doorway. The drizzle turned to rain. "Do you think Dad will come back, Sarah?" she asked me. "What does he mean by us dropping hints, anyway?"

"I think he wants us to say something to Mom every once in a while to let her know he's willing to talk about coming back."

"Why doesn't he just ask her?"

"You know as well as I do, Cori. Mom won't talk to him about it. She's still mad about how he just walked out without even trying to work things out. She says that wasn't fair to her and us kids. You've heard her say she's had it with Dad."

"Granny Rubin says Dad just needed a vacation," Cori said.

"I know. Maybe she's right, but Mom says she needed a vacation, too, and maybe they could have taken one together or something. I don't know, Cori. Maybe they'll work it out. It won't hurt to drop a hint to Mom. Anyway, we're big enough to look after ourselves now."

This wasn't really true. Cori was still a little kid in some ways. She needed to be reassured a lot or she'd begin to cry when nothing was wrong.

"I'm only nine," she said. "You're almost twelve, Sarah. The year after next you'll be going to high school. I still need help with my homework and I'd like to be a Girl Scout and things like that, that we don't have time for. It's not right we aren't a family anymore and I'm going to tell Dad about it."

"You have Cleaver, Cori," I teased her. "He looks after you, doesn't he?" Which was sort of true. Cleaver and Cori were a pair. He'd do things for her he wouldn't do for anyone else. At night he'd sneak up to her room to sleep beside her bed until Mom chased him back to the kitchen where he belonged.

Cori reached out her foot and tickled Cleaver in the stomach with her toes. Cleaver grunted and opened one eye for a minute. He was worn out from barking at the waves. Cori didn't say anything more. Even though Mom and I tried to make up for it, she missed Dad. He always used to fool around to make her laugh, doing things like throwing her in the air and catching her at the last second or chasing her around the counter with a broom, saying he was going to sweep her out the door with the rest of the trash.

I got up and reached down to pull Cori to her feet.

"We better go back. We're going to get soaked. Maybe Dad will leave early and take us to a movie. Come on, Cleaver, it's time to go."

Cleaver didn't budge. We left him there and walked down to the beach. When we reached the water, we heard him thundering after us. He didn't stop. He ran on toward Dad, who was just a spot in the rain way down the beach. We ran after him, kicking up spray when the waves washed in under our feet.

"It's an awful day for blues," Dad said. "We might as well pack up and head for home. I'll give it one more try, then we'll leave." He leaned back with the rod and threw the line out as far as it would go. He waited. Suddenly it tightened and the rod bent. "I got one," Dad shouted. "Look at him pull. It's a big one. We'll have him for supper." He began to reel the line in.

Cleaver watched Dad, wagging his tail at the excitement. When the fish came close to shore, it made a jump to shake the hook loose. Cleaver charged. Before Dad could drag the fish up on the beach, Cleaver grabbed it in his big mouth and started to run. Dad pulled back on the rod. Cleaver pulled in the other direction. The poor bluefish was struggling between Cleaver and Dad. Cori and I ran to rescue the fish. Just as we grabbed him, the hook came loose. The fish plopped down in the water and headed out to sea. Cleaver went after him, but it was too late. Dad stood there swearing under his breath at Cleaver and the fish.

"What do you suppose got into that stupid dog's head?" he asked us.

18

"I don't know, Dad," I said. "Cleaver doesn't like fish much."

"Yeah," Cori added. "Fish is about the only thing he doesn't like except chocolate ice cream."

Dad laughed. He gathered his gear and we walked up to the parking lot. "I'll stop at the fish house and buy a mess of blues for the freezer. Your mother doesn't have to know where they come from, does she?"

5

It was late when we got home Saturday night. The lights were still on in the diner. Linda had gone home. Granny Rubin and Mom were seated in a booth talking seriously. They looked worried. Cleaver thumped around the counter without a hello to anyone and collapsed. He was worn out from sniffing out the window all the way back. Dad put the blues in the freezer and started for the door.

"Just a minute, Ed," Mom said.

Dad stopped and turned around. He looked sort of hopeful. "Yes, Nettie?" he said.

"We have to talk about that black beast you dropped off here a year ago on your way out."

Dad looked puzzled. "What's the problem? Cleaver went with us. He stole the only fish I caught." He realized what he had just said and shut up.

"It's not what he did when he was with you; it's what

he did before he went, Thursday afternoon, to be exact, over at the playing field." Mom asked Cori, "Why didn't you tell me? And you, too, Sarah?"

Cori began to cry, the way she usually did when Mom was sharp with her. She didn't fight back with Mom. Granny Rubin pulled her over to the edge of her seat and put her arm around her. "It's not so bad, Nettie."

"Of course it's bad, Mama. We don't even have dog insurance. The donor forgot to send a policy along with the dog."

"Calm down, Nettie," Dad said, "and tell me what you're so upset about. Who did Cleaver bite, if that's what's wrong?"

"Teddy Bigby. I told Mrs. Bigby I'd have to talk to the girls before I discussed it any further with her. What happened at the playing field, Sarah?"

"Nothing, Mom, nothing I saw. Cleaver was with Cori. I was at the swings talking to Charlotte."

"Cori didn't tell you anything?"

"No, Mom."

"What happened, Cori?" Mom demanded. "Stop crying for a minute and tell me the truth."

"Nothing," Cori sobbed. "Teddy Bigby called me a name. I told him to stop. He kept on so I shoved him. He hit me and Cleaver grabbed his arm and wouldn't let go until I told him to."

"I said it wasn't anything serious, Nettie," Granny Rubin said. "Just a playground fight. That's nothing serious."

"Be quiet, Mama. Cori, listen to me. Mrs. Bigby said

21

Cleaver attacked Teddy and bit him on the arm and tore his new jacket. She said she was going to take Teddy to the doctor and was going to file a complaint against Cleaver with the police."

"It's not true, Mom. Cleaver didn't bite him. He just held on and growled a little bit. Teddy tore his own jacket climbing over the wire fence at the pond with David Fallon. I saw him. He told David his mother would kill him when she saw it."

"How come she didn't call Thursday when it happened?" Dad asked Mom.

"She said she waited to see how bad the bite was. By Friday afternoon it turned purple, she said. She also said she was thinking of suing us for damages."

Dad snorted, the way he did when he didn't like something.

"What did he call you, Cori?" Granny Rubin wanted to know. "Was it a bad name?"

"Yes."

"What was it? You can tell us."

"Corinthia," Cori whispered.

Granny Rubin's jaw dropped. "Corinthia? But that's your name."

Cori started to cry again. "I know it's my name, but I wish it wasn't."

Mom stared hard at Granny Rubin. "Well, Mama, that's what happens when you meddle in other people's business. Wasn't it enough to call me Benedicta and make me into a Nettie the rest of my life? Corinthia, what a name to load on a pretty little baby. You

22

should be out in Hollywood, Mama, making up names for all the new movie stars."

Mom and Dad had named me Sarah, which was a pretty good name, I guess, but it never satisfied Granny Rubin. She liked the fancy names she read in the ladies' magazines. She was always fussing about my being called Sarah when I could have been a Felicia or Damathine or Ramona. Grandpa used to tell her she should read the Bible if she wanted good names.

But Grandma Rubin had an answer to that. She pointed to Mom, who was really beautiful, even when she was tired and upset. "Look at Benedicta," she would say. "You want a woman like that to be a Rachel or Sharon or Ruth? Benedicta, Benedicta Rubin Stuart, that's a beautiful name for a beautiful daughter."

Mom would listen and shake her head. "What about Nettie?" she'd ask. "What about Nettie Rubin? That's a good name for a delicatessen."

"You should insist on Benedicta," Granny Rubin would reply. "That's your real name."

So when Cori was born, Granny Rubin was there to do the naming. Mom had a tough time having Cori and she was too tired to fight back when Granny Rubin told the nurses the baby's name was Corinthia. That's how it got put down and was never changed. Dad said he thought Mom and Granny Rubin liked it, so he didn't say anything.

Mom called the baby Cori right away and that's what stuck, but every once in a while a teacher would get it in her head she was Corinthia. The name spread and the kids saw that Cori didn't like it, so they teased her about it. Usually she ignored them, but sometimes she would fight back. Teddy Bigby was a nasty kid. Cori probably did shove him.

"But did you push him?" Mom insisted.

"Yes," Cori replied.

"Then he hit you. Where?" Mom went on.

"On the shoulder."

"And Cleaver bit his arm?"

"No," Cori shouted. "Cleaver held his arm, the way he does when he's playing. Cleaver wouldn't bite anyone."

"Mrs. Bigby said his arm is bruised and the skin almost broken."

"I don't know about that," Cori said. "Maybe he bruised it going over the fence. Teddy Bigby is a liar."

Dad spoke up. "I think Cori's right, Nettie. The kid tore his jacket and hurt his arm. He made up a story about the dog because he's afraid of his mother. She's a terror, they say. Poor old Charley Bigby is scared to go home after work. Let's leave it be and see what happens."

He headed for the door. He turned as he left. "It looks like I got you a good dog after all, Benedicta," he said, laughing.

Mom kissed Cori on top of the head. We went around the counter to see if Cleaver was all right. He opened one eye and wagged his tail to let us know he was just fine.

6

Mondays weren't much fun generally, especially if we'd had a good visit with Dad on the weekend or a special project with Mom that didn't include the diner, like going over to the ski tow in the winter. Mondays always meant school. Cori thought school was great, but I was getting tired of it.

This September we took the bus to school. I liked to walk, since it wasn't much over a mile. Usually I'd pick up someone along the way and we'd talk about what we did over the weekend unless Cori butted in. But Cleaver got so big over the summer we had to give up walking. If he saw us taking off down the path toward school, there was no longer any holding him. In the diner he'd run back and forth from the front door to the back door, trying to get out. When we tied him to the tree he set up a howl you could hear for miles around. Up in the house he crashed through the bottom screen on the screen door and tore down the hill after us. Granny Rubin followed him with a pan in her hand to whack him with, she was so mad about the hole in the screen.

But one day when we took the bus, which stopped right in front of the diner to let us on, Cleaver waited with us nice as could be. He wagged his tail at the driver, barked once to let us know he was all right, and went around to the back of the diner to lie down. Mom said he was crazy and Granny Rubin agreed. Dad said Cleaver was just one of those dogs who had to look after things and that included taking us to school if we walked. After that Mom made us take the bus.

That turned out all right. This year I made my first really good friend, Helen Yeng. She was born in Hong Kong and came here when she was little. Her father was the cook in the Chinese restaurant in the mall and her mother did sewing at the dry cleaner's next to the restaurant. Helen helped out in one place or the other every afternoon after school except Monday.

Monday was Helen's day to come home with me. It was a slow day at the Good Luck and Mom didn't need me. Helen and I went up to my room and talked or took Cleaver to the playing field or sat around in the empty diner trying to scrounge an extra soda from Mom.

This Monday, Mom was racking her brain over what to have for the Monday-night special. She sat down at the booth with us and drank a grape soda. "I don't know," she said to no one in particular, "what I'm doing in this business. I never liked to cook when I was growing up, sort of how you aren't interested in cooking now, Sarah. The only reason I learned was to help your father out when he was running behind. Now he's gone and I'm always running behind. What do you do in the Golden Dragon, Helen?"

"I help my father cook," Helen replied.

Mom's eyes lit up. "Do you think you could help me this afternoon with the Monday special? Just this once. After that I can make it myself whenever I need to."

I could see that Helen didn't think much of the idea. After all, her dad was in the same business over in the mall, except Chinese food was his business. If he found out Helen was helping us serve Chinese food every Monday in the diner, he might get mad at Helen.

Mom saw that, too, as soon as she spoke. "I'm sorry, Helen. It wouldn't be proper, I know."

But that wasn't it. "Oh, no, Mrs. Stuart, that is not the problem. I would be proud to help you, and my father would be proud of me for helping you. He thinks everyone should eat Chinese food. Even Cleaver." She reached down and scratched Cleaver's ears. He was lying at our feet waiting for his banana ice cream.

Helen explained that she wasn't sure Mom had the stuff she needed and she was afraid she would do a bad job and dishonor Chinese food and chase Mom's customers away.

"Well," Mom said, "why don't we go out in the

27

kitchen and see? If we don't have it, you can't do it, and we'll have meat loaf again."

Now Helen's eyes lit up. "Oh," she said, "I can make Chinese meat loaf. It's not really Chinese, but we eat it at home sometimes. My mother made it for my father and he called it Chinese meat loaf."

"What do you need?" Mom asked. "I have tons of hamburger meat."

"Soy sauce?" Helen asked.

"Yes."

"I can use spaghetti instead of Chinese noodles," Helen said to herself. "Hot chili sauce?"

Mom nodded.

"We can use marmalade for duck sauce," Helen went on. "Let's see what else."

I went around the counter to give Cleaver his dish of ice cream. When I came back, Helen and Mom were in the kitchen, chattering away. I felt left out. Mom had stolen my only friend. I yelled up the hill for Cori and we took Cleaver to the playing field. Teddy Bigby was there, too. He came up and apologized to Cori and gave Cleaver a pat on the head. He said his dad made him tell his mom the truth about Cleaver and the jacket. He said his mom was going to apologize to our mom, but Mrs. Bigby never did.

There was a wonderful smell in the diner when we got back. "Get your Magic Markers," Mom yelled at Cori. Cori was in charge of writing up the specials sheets to put in the menus and stick on the front door.

"What do you want me to write?" Cori yelled back.

Mom came to the serving window. "'Helen's Chinese Meat Loaf,'" she told Cori. "Write it in big red letters."

Cleaver was the first to try it when it came out of the oven all browned and round and smelling super-delicious. Mom mixed in a small slice with his dog food. But Cleaver knew what was what. He separated out the meat loaf and left the canned dog food in his dish to show Helen he had respect for Chinese food. When no one was looking, he ate the rest of his supper and went back under the counter.

7

The third Wednesday in October was the big field-hockey game with Upton Falls Junior High. No one seemed to know why it had to be on the third Wednesday in October, but it always was. It had something to do with a tradition. Our coach, Mrs. Rufino—she taught social science—said it had been that way when she came to Stanhope twenty-five years ago, and if she ever knew, she had forgotten. She told us we should pay attention to the game, not the date. Mrs. Rufino liked to win.

It was my first year on the team. Mrs. Rufino called me her star right wing. I wasn't much better than anyone else, I just worked harder. Mom told me during the summer that if I was serious about field hockey, I had better get ready, so Cori and I went to the playing field in the mornings, when there wasn't anybody there except a few people jogging around the track, and knocked the ball up and down the field. Cori was as good as I was, but they didn't let elementary-school kids play on the team.

Sometimes between the breakfast rush and lunch, Mom and Granny Rubin would walk Cleaver over to watch, leaving Linda in charge of the diner. They had to hold Cleaver pretty tight. Whenever he got loose he chased after us, snapping at the ball to start with, then grabbing it in his mouth and running around the field, his tail high, pretending he had just won the game. I practiced most of the summer.

Mrs. Rufino said this year's game was a must win. Upton Falls had won the big game for the last six years and Mrs. Rufino took those losses to heart. The team didn't really care that much, except for me—I sort of liked to win—but Mrs. Rufino was real nice and bought us double-dip ice-cream cones every time we won a game. We talked it over after practice Tuesday morning and decided to win the big game for Mrs. Rufino. We had already won five games without a loss and we felt pretty confident.

"Granny and I will be there, Sarah," Mom shouted as we went out to meet the school bus. "Remember to keep your head down the way Mrs. Rufino told you."

After school we changed into our blue uniforms and went out on the field so the Upton Falls kids could change. They had these horrible orange uniforms that made the girls look like some of the wrestlers Cori looked at on television. They called themselves the

Tigers. They marched over to their side of the field shouting, "We're number one. We're number one," and waving their index fingers in the air. I thought it was pretty stupid. It was only a field-hockey game, not the Super Bowl.

Usually no one showed up for our home games, just a few junior-high kids who lived in town and didn't have to take the bus home. But Wednesday there must have been a hundred people standing along our sideline cheering for us. A lot of cars came over from Upton Falls, too, with orange banners stuck on their car aerials. Kids carried a big sign: WE'RE NUMBER ONE. They hadn't lost a game, either, so I suppose it was a big game.

It went back and forth in the middle of the field most of the time, neither team getting much of a chance to score. The Upton Falls girls played dirty. They tripped and didn't care if they whacked you really hard with their hockey sticks. Mrs. Rufino was furious. She shouted at the referee that she should call the orange team for fouling, but the referee didn't pay any attention. Ruthie Pound said the referee lived in Upton Falls; she was a friend of Ruthie's mother.

Late in the second half, when the sun was slipping behind the sugar maples, the game was still scoreless. The girls in orange seemed to be getting tired, maybe from all their shouting about being number one. Mrs. Rufino sent in a substitute to tell us to go on the attack, we could win. We started pressing and pushing them back. When we were close to their goal, I managed to get clear. Their goalie was too far out. Sue Watkins made a perfect pass over to me. I pulled my hockey stick back to knock the ball in when a big, black-and-white shape charged in front of me, grabbed the ball in his big mouth, and ran across the field to the Upton Falls sideline, his tail up and waving like crazy.

Linda had made a bad mistake. Cleaver wouldn't have left the diner in the middle of the afternoon without his ice cream if it had caught fire and burned down. Generally he flopped under the counter, his chin on the floor between his paws, watching us until someone headed for the freezer with a dish in her hand. Linda said later Cleaver was acting peculiar that afternoon. He must have figured none of us was around to give him his ice cream, so he paced up and down behind the counter getting in Linda's way. He was such a pest Linda decided she'd better give him his banana ice cream. She said he slurped it down in half a second and headed for the front door of the diner. He got there just as old Mr. Thompson opened it to come in for his early supper. He almost knocked poor Mr. Thompson over as he beat it down the steps for the playing field. He arrived just in time to save the game for Upton Falls.

I chased after him. The whole blue team chased after Cleaver while the Upton Falls team stood around laughing and cheering. He ran from one side of the field to the other, growling under his breath when any of us came too close. Then he started running from goal to goal, dodging in and out between the two teams. Mom and Cori, even the referee, joined the chase. I could hear Granny Rubin screaming at Cleaver in German from the sidelines. It didn't do much good. Cleaver didn't understand German very well.

Eventually he got tired of the game. He escaped under the Upton Falls goal and lay down, the ball between his legs. He let me take it. I gave it to the referee. She looked at her watch and threw up her arm. "Time," she shouted. "Nothing to nothing," as if we didn't already know.

The orange team was glad to get away with a tie. They gave us a little cheer and ran into the locker room, still laughing.

Our team was pretty mad at Cleaver and me. "That stupid dog kept us from winning," Sue Watkins said in a loud voice. "I could have scored, Sarah, if I hadn't passed it over to you. You let that awful dog grab it." Terry Dunne said, "That isn't so, Sue." I didn't answer. I sat next to Cleaver and cried.

Mrs. Rufino came over and sat down beside me. She patted Cleaver on the head. He licked her hand to show he was sorry for causing all the trouble. Mrs. Rufino put her arm around me. "Don't feel bad, Sarah. It's only a game. Anyway, we sort of won. Cleaver made the only goal and he's on our team. Come on, let's go change and have some ice cream."

8

The next morning I didn't feel like going to school. Cori went down to the diner to tell Mom I wasn't feeling well. Mom came up the hill to take a look. "Where do you feel bad, Sarah?" she said. "Tummy or head?"

"I don't know, Mom. I just feel bad all over. I think I ought to stay in bed today."

Mom felt my head and told me I didn't have a fever. She brought me an aspirin and a glass of water from the bathroom and sat on the edge of the bed while I swallowed the pill. "You don't want to go to school because you're ashamed of what Cleaver did yesterday and you're afraid the kids will laugh at you, is that it, Sarah?"

When something like yesterday happened, things got all mixed up in my head. I'd felt this way before—not really caring what happened. Mom said it was depression and wanted to take me to a doctor. Granny Rubin said wait. I heard them talking one night downstairs. "Wait awhile, Benedicta," Granny Rubin had said. "Bad things are happening to her, but she has to deal with them herself. What's a doctor going to tell her, Benedicta? Sarah will be all right. She's a healthy girl, she'll be all right. Just be patient. You think maybe Abram and I didn't go through this with you? Look at you now."

"Yeah, look at me," Mom said. "Almost forty years old, half-divorced, working myself to death sixteen hours a day in a diner."

Granny Rubin sounded the way she did when she didn't like what you said. "You have two fine girls, Benedicta. You have your health and you own a business. And we both know Ed is coming back."

So I didn't want to cause Mom any trouble Thursday morning. I mentioned that I just didn't feel all that great.

But Mom was worried and she didn't give up.

"Cleaver's only a dog, Sarah. He didn't know it was so important for you girls to win. The kids will laugh at him, not you."

"Maybe, Mom, but somebody might say something and I'll start to cry or get mad. I'd like to stay home today."

Mom stood up. The mornings were always busy at the Good Luck Diner. That was when the delivery-truck drivers had their breakfast before they started out. "I have to go down the hill now. I think I know how you feel. When your father went away, I felt like the whole town was watching and talking about me and maybe laughing at me for not holding on to my husband. Of course, they weren't. Nobody cared except us. Is something else bothering you, too?"

"No, Mom. If I feel better I'll get up and walk to school."

Granny Rubin came in when Mom left. She was in her old housecoat and slippers, her gray hair held back with one of my elastics. She was seventy-five years old and she said it took a little while now to get started in the morning. She looked after the house until noon. Then she went down to take over the register. Sometimes she'd spell Linda behind the counter.

"I've been listening to you and your mother," she said. "You have problems?" Granny Rubin had only a little bit of accent, unless she was upset, like Wednesday afternoon when she was yelling at Cleaver.

It was easier talking to her than to Mom. "A couple, I guess," I answered.

She puckered up her lips and looked at me hard. "It's not that crazy Cleaver, is it, child?"

"Not really, I suppose. It's a lot of things. It's just that Cleaver brought attention to me. I don't like the kids to pay attention to me."

"You're ashamed of something, Sarah?"

"Maybe. I'm not sure."

"Like your mother and father being separated, that makes you feel you don't belong?"

"Sort of, but lots of kids have parents separated or divorced."

"And like maybe you have to work in the diner some afternoons and evenings, that, too, Sarah?"

"That, too, Granny Rubin."

"But that's not it, either, is it?"

"Not really."

"It's because half your family is Jewish, maybe? Is that it, Sarah?"

That was it, but I didn't want to say so. Every once in a while somebody would say something nasty to Cori and me, not often, but whenever they did, we didn't know what to say back. There weren't many Jewish or half-Jewish families in Stanhope; we felt that we stuck out because we were different somehow, along with the diner and the separation and Cleaver causing trouble. It seemed that Cori and I spent most of our time trying not to call attention to ourselves.

Granny Rubin stopped asking questions. She took my hand and held it in her lap. Then she asked, "You feel ashamed of your mother and Grandpa Rubin and me, is that it?"

"No," I said loudly. "No, you know that's not so."

"You feel a little ashamed of yourself?" Granny Rubin persisted. "You mustn't take the blame for your family, Sarah."

I had never thought of it that way. I guess Cori and I were ashamed of ourselves because we felt our family was different.

"Your mother's Jewish. Your grandparents are Jewish. We don't go to synagogue, maybe because they don't have one for us in Stanhope, but we're Jewish all right. Once we were German and Jewish, now we're

38

American and Jewish. Your father is American and not much of anything else, but that doesn't matter, either. You and Cori are stuck with your parents, Sarah, but you don't have to feel ashamed about it. You've done better than most kids in getting a good mom and dad."

She was quiet again. She squeezed my hand in an absentminded way. She looked at me harder.

"Listen to me, Sarah. I want to tell you something. Your mother said I shouldn't talk about the old country much because it might upset you and Cori and I should tell you later or whenever you asked. But maybe I won't be around later, like my Abram isn't around now, and it's something you should know.

"We came to this country fifty years ago, when I was twenty-five and Grandpa Rubin was thirty. We didn't really come. You could say we escaped. The two of us managed to get to England and some people there helped us get to America. Grandpa went to work in the piano factory. Ten years later your mother was born. That was all the family we had until you and Cori came along. The rest of our relatives are gone."

"You mean they're all dead?" I asked.

"I mean they were all killed."

Granny Rubin saw I didn't understand. "Our families made your grandfather and me leave. Grandpa had been beat up and badly hurt. They made us leave. They didn't leave because they didn't want to or couldn't. A little while after that they were taken away and killed by the Germans. We never heard from them."

"Why?"

"Only God knows why. The Germans said it was because we were Jews. We were different, and they said we were too dangerous to have around."

"Would they have killed you and Grandpa Rubin?" I wanted to know.

"Yes. They had started before we left. They told us we weren't Germans. We had to wear a Star of David when we went outside. We had to stay away from Germans. Your grandfather lost his job. Some of us were put in jail. Our houses were destroyed. Germans were afraid to speak to us. Then the soldiers took all the Jews away."

"Were you ashamed of being Jewish?"

"Yes, the Germans made me ashamed. People said things to me and I was ashamed and afraid. Even when we came here I was still ashamed. Your grandfather wasn't afraid. He was proud of what he was. You know what he said, Sarah, when we called it the Good Luck Diner and Deli? He said, 'That will tell people we're American and we're Jewish!' That's what you are. Sarah, you should be proud of it." Granny Rubin let go of my hand and stood up to leave.

"I guess I better go to school now," I said to her, "or I'll miss field-hockey practice."

"Good," Granny Rubin told me. "You get dressed and brush your hair. I'll make you apple pancakes like the ones my mother used to make for me in the old country."

9

Linda had been moping around the diner since college started in early September. She was pleasant to the customers and Mom, but she snapped at Cori and me, even Cleaver once or twice, when we got in the way behind the counter. Mom noticed but she didn't say anything. She was fond of Linda and used to say Linda was her third daughter. It was Granny Rubin who came right out and asked Linda what was the matter. Linda muttered something about not wanting to go back to school. Granny Rubin didn't believe that for a minute. She told Mom it was something else. She was right, the way she usually was when she nosed into somebody else's business. One afternoon when Linda took two hours off to go to the dentist, Granny Rubin had a talk with Mom about Linda. Cori and I listened in. "I told you there was something wrong, Benedicta, and there is. What is wrong is that no-good Gary Weems. He's after Linda to marry him."

"That's silly," Mom said. "Linda's too smart to get married. She has to finish school first. Anyway, how do you know so much about it?"

"How else?" Granny Rubin answered. "I asked her and she told me, that's how I know." Granny Rubin was pretty proud of herself for getting to the bottom of the Linda problem.

Gary Weems was a big, blond guy from Madison. Linda had met him in her first year at the college. He drove a bulldozer in the summer and made a lot of money. He bought a black Trans Am with a golden eagle on the door. He'd storm into the parking lot at nine o'clock some evenings, slam on the brakes, and blow the horn good and loud for Linda. That made Mom mad, but she didn't say anything because she liked Linda a lot and she also needed her. Linda had been working in the Good Luck Diner and Deli since she was a junior in high school. At first she worked in the evenings from five to eight, but when she started college she came in at noon and worked till almost nine. In the summers she worked all day. Clair—Mrs. Muldowney—did the morning shift. She had to leave at noon to pick up her kid at kindergarten. She couldn't work in the summer. Mom said Linda was the best there was, quick, smart, friendly. She made a lot of tips. She never said how much, but one evening Cori sneaked a look in her cigar box and counted up to eighteen dollars before Linda came back and chased her away.

Mom didn't waste any time. As soon as Linda came back from the dentist, Mom asked her what her intentions were. "I have to know," Mom said. "It's going to be hard to get anyone half as good as you are, not to mention as reliable. And I have to start right away if you're thinking of leaving."

Linda got all flustered, the way she did when she mixed up her orders, which wasn't very often. "Gee, I don't know, Mrs. Stuart. Gary keeps talking about getting married now and maybe moving to Florida or California where he can work the year round."

Linda had told us, when we asked about Gary, that he wasn't doing so well in school. He went only because his folks were paying for it and there wasn't much work around for a bulldozer driver in the winter. He had flunked Spanish and gotten a D in English at the end of his first year, and the college had put him on probation.

"You're giving up on being a teacher, Linda?" Mom asked.

"Gee, I don't know, Mrs. Stuart," Linda said again. "After I finish at the college, I'll have to go to school another year to get my accreditation, and it's hard to get a teaching job these days. I'm sort of discouraged. My folks want me to go on. My mother says she'll take a job to help pay for tuition if I want to quit working here for a while, but that doesn't seem right. She still has to look after my two brothers. I think maybe I should give you notice now, so you can start to find someone else. Maybe I can go to school in Florida or

California once we're settled in. I'm sorry, Mrs. Stuart. You've been real good to me here in the diner."

I guess Mom didn't see any point in arguing with Linda, the way Granny Rubin would have done. "People have to make their own mistakes," she said. "I've made enough of my own." She asked Linda if she thought her mother would like to work in the diner. Linda said she thought not, her mother had trouble with her ankles.

Cori and I had been listening to the discussion, pretending to wipe the counter and get the setups on and sweep around under the stools. Linda was almost family. She stopped to help us when we were behind with the dirty dishes or dipping up the ice cream. I'd ask Linda, not Mom, when I had a problem with schoolwork. She always found time to give me the answer.

"Are you really going to leave?" Cori asked as soon as Linda came back to change the coffee filter.

"I guess so, Cori."

"Do you really love Gary Weems?" Cori went on. "I don't think he's so hot. Maybe you could do better if you waited." Cori always spoke her mind. She had noticed that Gary almost never spoke to her when he came into the diner.

"I do love him, Cori. He's not so bad when you get to know him. And he truly loves me. It wouldn't be so bad not to have to work for a while."

"That's what Mom says, too," Cori remarked. "I'm not going to hang around the diner when I grow up. I'm going to be an actress on television."

I didn't say anything. I would miss Linda Kowelski. She was like a big sister to me. And I was sure Cleaver would miss her. She liked him almost as much as she said she loved Gary Weems. That's what she told him one afternoon when he put his head in her lap and looked lonely like he did when he wanted attention.

After that, things were pretty busy and we forgot about Linda's going away. Mom looked a little more upset than usual out in the kitchen, but she smiled every time she took an order over to the window for Linda.

A little after nine, the Trans Am roared up to the side of the diner, brakes biting into the asphalt. There was a blast on the horn. Linda wasn't quite ready. She stuck her head out the door and told Gary to wait a minute, she'd be right there. Cleaver came out from behind the counter to say good-bye to Linda. He did that whenever he heard the Trans Am's horn.

Linda didn't seem to be in her usual hurry to leave. Cori and I watched her as she fiddled around counting her tips and putting on her jacket. Gary gave another blast on his horn. Linda bit her lower lip. She was cross with him, we could see. As she walked slowly over to the door, there was still another blast, a long one, and a car door slammed. Gary thumped up the steps. Linda told Cleaver good-bye. She bent over to give him a kiss on the white spot on his head. She went out the door. When she was outside and her back was turned, Gary Weems reached in with his foot and kicked Cleaver in the jaw. He'd never liked Cleaver because Cleaver wouldn't shake with him when Gary told him to. He was polite enough, but you could see he didn't like Gary much.

Cleaver gave a big yip and ran back to the counter. We heard some loud talk outside. Then the Trans Am started up and spun its tires out to the road. Linda came back into the diner and sat down. She put her arms around Cleaver and hugged him tight. Tears rolled down her face.

Then Linda walked over to the window. "Could I take my notice back, Mrs. Stuart? I think maybe I better finish school after all."

Mom came out of the kitchen. She was smiling and crying at the same time. She hugged Linda and told Cori to give Cleaver a big dish of banana ice cream.

10

Out in back of our house was a barn that was falling down. Mom used to play there when she was growing up. Then the roof started leaking and one side started sagging; Cori and I were told to stay out because there was no telling when the whole building might fall down. After he finished putting the addition on the house, Dad said he'd start on the barn. He never got around to it; he was too busy in the kitchen of the Good Luck Diner.

Cori and I would sneak out to the barn sometimes and poke around. It wasn't much of a barn, just a big shack, really, with a hayloft we didn't dare climb up to. Other kids had trunks full of old clothes and furniture and dead cars in their barns, if they had one. We didn't have anything except for the swallows' nests up on the rafters. That is, until the raccoons moved in.

There were plenty of raccoons in Stanhope—too many, most people said. They lived in the town forest on the other side of our hill and ate out of our garbage cans whenever they were hungry. Mom said it would be easier to put out a plate of scraps than to clean the mess every time the coon family raided the garbage cans. No matter what we did, they managed to get the tops off and help themselves, especially if they smelled fish bones inside. Dad used to leave the fish scraps outside, but Mom didn't believe in leaving garbage outside the cans. Coons were all right, maybe—they were sort of cute, she said—but rats would be next.

During the winter one of the raccoon families gave up walking over the hill for a late supper and moved into a corner of the barn. We didn't know that until we were exploring out there in the spring and found four little raccoons huddled up against one another. The mother wasn't around. We ran down to the diner and brought up Mom and Granny Rubin, and afterward Linda, to see the babies. "What next?" Mom said. "We'll have a zoo here before long." Cori wanted to try feeding them, but when we told Dad about the coon family, he said we should leave them alone and only take a look when their mother wasn't around. "Raccoons, even babies, can be nasty. They bite and scratch. They'll go away when they get bigger. Raccoons are smarter than most animals—except for Cleaver. They know when to leave."

We kept Cleaver away from the barn. He wasn't much interested in it, anyway, since there was nothing to eat there. He preferred the diner. Sure enough, Dad was right. The babies grew bigger and friskier. One of them ran across Cori's sneakers and made her scream. Then they disappeared. Dad said they might come back in the winter, but you couldn't count on it.

Cleaver went out to the barn with us one day after the raccoons had left and sniffed where they had been. He was all excited about having some playmates out back and tried to track them down. Cleaver had a good nose, but he couldn't follow them. Still, he'd go out to the barn every once in a while to check up. When we called him, he'd sneak out the barn door looking sheepish. He knew he wasn't supposed to go in the barn any more than we were.

What Cori and I didn't know—Cleaver, either, I guess—was that some other animals had moved into the barn when the weather turned raw. One morning when we let Cleaver out, he went to have another look inside the barn. Granny Rubin was standing at the kitchen door to let him back in to have his oatmeal when she saw Cleaver charge out of the barn shaking all over. He rolled in the grass and rubbed his face in the ground. Then he ran down the hill to the diner as fast as he could go. Granny Rubin said he didn't go to the back door the way he was supposed to and knock with his left paw for someone to let him in. He went around to the front door, which he could push open with his nose. That's what he did. Granny Rubin asked us what had gotten into Cleaver.

It was close to eight o'clock and every stool in the

diner was taken, even a couple of the booths, by people on their way to work, mostly truck drivers. Many of them knew Cleaver and, when Clair wasn't looking, gave him a piece of bacon or the last bite of a doughnut. Cleaver had a lot of friends who came to the diner every morning.

But not that morning. None of his friends was glad to see him. The smell of Cleaver's new friend up in the barn had them heading for the door in thirty seconds. They told Clair they'd pay her the next day. Within a minute the diner was empty, plates of half-eaten food and cups of hot coffee sitting there on the counter. Only Cleaver was left, wondering where everybody went.

Mom was the last to get a whiff of him. When she stuck her head out the window she got a better whiff. "Good heavens," she yelled. "That's the last thing we needed. What were you messing with a skunk for, you stupid dog?"

Cleaver felt so ashamed and upset he followed her straight out the back door and let her tie him to the maple tree without a fight. She went back in and turned off the stove. She opened both doors and threw up the windows. After that, she used up two cans of disinfectant spray. It was noon before Mom let anyone in to eat.

When Granny Rubin and I found out what happened, I called Dad right away at the launderette, where he was every morning, cleaning up and checking the machines.

He laughed and said that would teach Cleaver not to mess around with skunks. "Maybe he's not as smart as a raccoon, after all," he said. "I'd come over and help, but your mother would probably take after me with a pan. Fill up Cori's plastic pool and put lots of vinegar and tomato juice in the water. Wear old clothes, because you're going to end up smelling like Cleaver. Use a strong soap."

One good thing about Cleaver was that he liked to take a bath. He was proud of his white vest and plumed tail. We filled up the pool with the garden hose. Granny Rubin heated some water on the stove and poured it into the pool so Cleaver wouldn't get a chill. Then we dumped in three bottles of vinegar and two big cans of tomato juice. We scrubbed him for an hour. Mom came up twice to give us instructions. The second time she broke down and laughed at poor Cleaver because he looked so mournful and bedraggled, shivering in Cori's Mickey Mouse pool.

Granny Rubin helped us dry him off with fluffy towels. He was so wet he let us use the hair blower. We changed our clothes and started off to school while Granny Rubin finished drying him. When he went down to the diner to take his nap under the counter, Mom said he smelled like a pickle.

Cleaver didn't go near the barn again. When Cori and I went to check, the skunks had cleared out, too. "That's too bad," Cori said. "I wanted to see what their babies looked like." Sometimes Cori could be as dumb as the dog.

11

Late in November the flu season started. Mom was the first to come down with it. She was running a fever before we finished Saturday night. Linda helped her up to the house and Granny Rubin put her to bed. Linda and Cori and I closed up.

"I'll come by tomorrow morning and help clean up," Linda promised. "I have a date tonight."

"Do you have a new boyfriend?" I asked.

"Maybe. I'm going to find out tonight," she said, laughing.

"What's his name?" Cori wanted to know.

"Mark."

"Mark what?" I asked.

"That's all I'm going to tell you right now," Linda replied. Since her fight with Gary Weems, she hadn't talked much about boyfriends. "Cori, you make a sign, your mother said—'Closed due to illness'—and tape it to the door."

"No sign," Granny Rubin said Sunday morning. "I have a better idea." She called up Dad and told him Mom was sick and a lot of good food would go to waste unless he took over in the kitchen for a while.

Dad wanted to know if that was what Mom wanted. Granny Rubin said Mom was too sick to know what she wanted.

Dad showed up Sunday afternoon and finished the cleaning job. He brought a couple of cookbooks. Afterward, he sat at the counter studying them. Cleaver lay at his feet looking happy that Dad was back. I was pretty happy, too. Cori was up in the house amusing Mom.

"What the Good Luck needs, Sarah, is more variety in its menu."

"Mom says she doesn't have time to learn new recipes. She has enough trouble keeping up with the old ones."

"Maybe so, but this week we're going to have some new specials. Like some Chinese dishes to go with Helen's meat loaf you told me about. And some Mexican food. There's a taco place in Madison that's always crowded. I'll buy a lot of beans and frozen tortillas and hot sauce. The other ingredients we have. Let's see what we'll have on Wednesday." He turned the pages of *Recipes from Around the World.*

"Mom's not going to think much of this, Dad."

"What she doesn't know won't hurt her. Granny

Rubin swore us all to secrecy. Your mother needs a good rest. It's hard to run a diner all the time. Launderettes aren't half the problem diners are." He went on reading. "I think Wednesday we'll have chicken cacciatore."

Helen and Dad hit it off right away. Dad hauled in a lot of Chinese stuff from Madison. He told Cori to make a sign. HELEN YENG'S MONDAY SPECIAL. They served up spicy pork with string beans, sweet-and-sour bluefish, mandarin chicken with mushrooms and water chestnuts. People must have gone and told their friends, because the diner was packed right up through nine o'clock. Tuesday afternoon Dad dragged me into the kitchen and we cooked Mexican. Cori made another sign. SEÑORITA SARAH'S MEXICAN SPECIAL. Mexican food wasn't all that hard to prepare, I discovered. Half the stuff came frozen. Once you got the hang of stuffing the tortillas and rolling them shut or making them stay bent over, that's about all there was to do except melt the cheese and shred the lettuce. We didn't have as many customers as Monday night, but everyone said the special was great.

"What about me?" Cori asked Dad. "All I do is make signs. What can I make?"

"I've been waiting for you to ask, Cori. I knew you would, sooner or later, so I laid in a case of frozen strawberries. We'll have Cori's Strawberry Shortcake Special to go with my chicken casserole. Sarah can make the signs."

Cori was as happy as a clam. Mom kept her out of

the kitchen. She said she could get burned. Dad let her do it all. She put too much sugar in the shortcake and splattered the whole kitchen whipping the cream, but it came out pretty well, considering it was Cori's first try. There was only a tiny bit left for Cleaver. Thursday it was Mom's macaroni dish, which was a favorite. Mom's fever went down and she was antsy about getting back down the hill. Saturday was the last college football game of the season. She said it would be a good time to open up again. She planned to go to the diner Friday evening to get ready.

"We'll have the regular frozen-fish special Friday night," Dad said. "That's no trouble. I want to prepare something really special for your mother. We'll all have a late dinner like they do in Paris."

He made Granny Rubin promise to keep Mom up in the house until nine o'clock. Dad set to work taking care of the lunch customers with one hand and preparing Mom's special dinner with the other.

At a quarter to nine the diner was empty. We put up the CLOSED sign. Linda put a white tablecloth on the table in the rear booth. Then she stuck a candle in a wine bottle and lit it. Dad brought out some French bread wrapped in a white napkin in a basket.

Linda would sit with me on one side. Granny Rubin and Cori would sit on the other side. Dad put a chair at the end of the booth for Mom. When Cleaver came by to see what was going on, Dad tied a dish towel around his neck and told him to sit.

Cori put a menu on each plate. She had used all the

colors in her Magic Marker set. It was a red, blue, green, orange, purple, and yellow menu.

GOOD LUCK DINER AND DELI
FRENCH SPECIAL
1. Onion Soup
2. Shrimp Quiche
3. Veal Orloff with Wild Rice
Salad with Stuart Dressing   Bread and Sweet Butter
Dessert—Chocolate Mousse
Assorted Wines and Soft Drinks

Dad went back into the kitchen. Linda turned the lights down. Granny Rubin brought Mom in. She had on her work clothes. When she saw the candle and the fancy booth setup she was so surprised she let Granny Rubin shove her into the chair before she said anything.

"What's going on?" she demanded.

We didn't answer. Dad came out in a stupid chef's hat with a tray of onion-soup bowls. "Voilà," he said, and served the soup.

"What kind of foolish game is this, Ed?" Mom asked.

Dad put his finger to his lips like a real French chef to tell Mom to keep quiet and eat.

Mom glared at Granny Rubin, who didn't pay any attention. She turned to Linda next. "I suppose he's been out there cooking all week, is that right, Linda?"

Linda nodded. She didn't say anything. Mom asked Cori and me some questions next. All we said was

"Yes, Mom" or "No, Mom," the way Dad told us to answer.

At the end of the meal, when Dad was taking the dessert plates off the table, Mom started to cry. She looked up at Dad with tears on her face and said, "That was lovely, Ed. Thank you."

Dad took off his chef's hat and bowed low to Mom. "My pleasure, madame," he said, and gathered up the dessert plates and took them into the kitchen.

Mom grabbed Cori and me by the hand and we headed up to the house. It was real late. "Off to bed with you," she said. "Tomorrow is a big day."

12

Stanhope wasn't a very big town. Even at the mall they pulled the sidewalks in at ten o'clock. The only place kids could go if they wanted to stay out was over to Madison, or farther, to New Haven or Hartford, both of them an hour away. Linda said the students at the college complained about what a hick town Stanhope was. Mom said no one made them come to college in a dead town. Granny Rubin said students should worry more about their lessons these days than having fun. The weekend before Thanksgiving was the big fall dance. Linda was going with Mark, she told us. She still wasn't sure Mark was her regular boyfriend, but she was pretty interested in him. She told Mom some of her friends had asked her if Mom could keep the diner open until three o'clock in the morning after the Saturday dance, which was over at midnight. They were willing to pay for the service, in addition to whatever food they bought.

The diner had a twenty-four-hour permit to stay open. Grandpa and Dad never kept the Good Luck open after nine o'clock because they found out there wasn't that much late-night business and there wasn't any help in Stanhope who wanted to sit up all night in an empty diner.

"I don't know why not," Mom replied. She really wanted to keep Linda around for another couple of years. "I suppose Sarah and I can take care of it and sleep late on Sunday. Would you and Mark be willing to come in for a couple of hours Sunday afternoon to help clean up? I'll put a service charge on for just enough to pay you both."

"That's all right, Mrs. Stuart. You don't have to pay us," Linda protested.

"But I want to," Mom answered. She and Dad both believed in paying people for what they did, unless it happened to be Cori and me. Mom said if people didn't need the money they wouldn't be working.

There was another matter she wanted to get straight. "No alcohol, not even beer, Linda. I don't have a license for alcohol or special parties. All I have is the twenty-four-hour permit, do you understand?"

Linda said she understood. She and Mark would tell their friends that if they wanted to drink, they had to do it somewhere else. Anyone who showed up drunk would have to leave. She asked Mom if it was all right to bring a stereo and some cassettes. Mom said fine if they didn't play it too loud.

As an extra precaution, Mom called up Chief Pettigrew to tell him what she was doing. He promised to have a police car drive by a couple of times and have an officer stop in for a cup of coffee to check up. Dance weekends could be pretty wild sometimes, he told her.

Cori, Mom, and I sat around Saturday night waiting for the fun to begin. Cori could stay up until things got started, then she had to go off to bed. Cleaver sat up with us. He was confused about what was going on. By ten o'clock every night he was under Granny Rubin's kitchen table, waiting to sneak up to Cori's room when the lights went out.

A little after midnight, Mark and Linda led a caravan of about twenty-five cars to the Good Luck Diner and Deli. Mom had left the sign on. Mark was in his tuxedo, and Linda was really beautiful in a white dress. Mark shook hands with all of us, including Cleaver, and set up the stereo. Cori whispered he wasn't as big as Gary Weems, but a lot better looking. Mark put Cori in charge of the boombox. She could turn it down if it was too loud. Mom went to the kitchen and I took orders behind the counter. Cleaver was interested in what was going on, but he stayed out of the way. There wasn't much room to dance in the middle of the diner. The students took turns dancing and eating. Most of the orders were for hamburgers and fries with Cokes or coffee. When Linda told her friends about Mom's super pepperoni-and-jalapeño-cheese sub, some people switched over.

About one-thirty, two late arrivals showed up, a guy big enough to be a football player or one of Cori's TV wrestlers and a spoiled-looking girl with her hair piled up on top of her head and a lot of jewelry. Neither one of them was walking very straight. The girl hung on to the boy for balance. Linda brought them over to the counter and found them two stools. She shook her head and rolled her eyes to tell me they were drunk and what could she do. I didn't think she or Mark wanted to tangle with the big guy.

"Why don't you get Stan and his friend some coffee?" Linda said to me.

Stan said in a loud voice he didn't want coffee. He wanted a beer, make that two beers, one for himself and one for Kim. "Isn't that right, Kim?" Kim said that was right.

"I'm sorry, we don't serve beer," I told them.

"What do you mean you don't serve beer? I want a can of beer and a big steak this thick." He showed me with his thumb and forefinger that he wanted a two-inch steak.

"I have to ask the cook if she has one that thick." I didn't say the cook was my mother.

"You do that, little girl, and be quick about it. We're as hungry as a couple of bears, aren't we, Kim?"

Kim said they were. I told Mom that Stan and Kim were pretty drunk and wanted beer and a couple of two-inch steaks.

"I don't have any steak that thick. If they cause trouble, ask Mark and Linda to make them leave."

Stan wasn't happy when I said we only had one-inch steaks. Did he want two of them and how did he want them?

Stan leaned over the counter. In an ugly tone he said, "I don't want a one-inch steak, little girl. I'm a two-inch steak man. Two of them, rare, and we want them fast, and two beers."

It was time to talk with Mark and Linda. They were dancing pretty close together at the back of the diner; I could see that Linda was keeping a worried eye on Stan. I pushed my way over to them and said I didn't know what to do with their friends.

"They're not our friends, Sarah. I don't know what they're doing here. We'll get rid of them."

Mark wasn't half as big as Stan, but he went right up behind him and tapped him politely on the shoulder. Stan turned around on his stool. "What do you want? Have you got the beer?"

Mark told him he would have to leave and take his girlfriend with him if she wanted to go. He was nice and firm about it. Stan laughed and put his foot up in Mark's stomach and shoved him hard, back into the crowd. Everyone was quiet. Cori turned off the boombox.

Mom came out of the kitchen with a heavy pan in her hand. Cleaver followed her. She marched right up to Stan. "You're drunk," she said. "We don't serve drunks here. Please leave."

Stan laughed right in Mom's face. "You're the cook in this greasy spoon, are you? You go back and fix my steak and another one for Kim; rare, both of them."

"You are not eating here. Please leave, both of you."

Stan said a couple of bad words and gave Mom a shove with his hand. She fell back against Linda, who kept her from falling to the floor. Stan laughed some more.

Suddenly he stopped laughing and howled and howled again. Then he screamed and hopped around on one leg. We heard a deep, fierce growl. Cleaver had taken a nip at Stan's leg. He hadn't just held on, the way he'd done with Teddy Bigby. He had sunk his teeth in.

Stan put both feet on the ground and aimed a kick at Cleaver's head. He lost his balance and fell down. Cleaver leaned over him and growled deep in his throat. Cori jumped off her stool and tried to pull Cleaver away. Cleaver wouldn't pull. He put his paws on Stan's chest and showed Stan most of his teeth.

Kim started to yell for help at the very moment when Chief Pettigrew dropped by for his coffee. He wanted to know what was going on. Mom told Cleaver to let Stan get up and he did. Stan got up and, muttering some more bad words, put his foot on the stool to look at his ankle. He was bitten, all right. You could see Cleaver's teeth marks above his ankle. They were red, but the skin wasn't broken.

Chief Pettigrew asked Mom and me what had happened. We told him. Mark and Linda and some of their friends told him the same thing. Then he asked Stan, who yelled about rabies and how Cleaver should be shot as a mad dog. Kim said the same thing.

Chief Pettigrew took Stan by the arm. "Come down to the station and we'll talk," he said.

"What are you going to do about the mad dog?" Stan shouted, calling Cleaver some bad names. "Anyway, what do we have to talk about? Tell me that."

"I'm going to do something about the dog right now," Chief Pettigrew said. He bent over and patted Cleaver's ribs. "You're a good dog, Cleaver." Then he said, "Come along, Stan. Let's go to the station and talk about being drunk and disorderly and causing a disturbance and using a dangerous weapon. That's your foot, Stan. Then we'll talk about getting your girlfriend home while you spend the night in jail."

13

Mom and Dad had always closed the Good Luck on Thanksgiving Day, and the whole family would go for dinner in the dining room of the Stanhope Hotel. Dad said the food wasn't so good, but the service was a lot better. Last year we put up the CLOSED sign and Mom, Cori, and I stayed home to eat Granny Rubin's roast turkey. Mom thought she'd do the same thing again, but the people who ran the rest home down the road asked her if she would prepare a Thanksgiving dinner for the old people who stayed there. Some of them came down during the week for supper at the diner. They all agreed they'd rather eat at the Good Luck this year than at the hotel. Thanksgiving dinner was a special occasion for them.

Mom didn't think much of the idea. She liked to get out of the kitchen on holidays. She agreed for one time only. "If I look after the rest-home folks now, maybe they'll look after me later on," she groaned to Granny Rubin.

When Dad heard that the diner was going to be open, he told us to ask Mom if he could take us up to Maine with him for Thanksgiving. He knew where we could get some lobsters cheap. Dad and Cori were crazy about lobsters. We asked Mom. She didn't think it was such a great idea. "I'll have to talk to your father about that," she said.

She didn't have to call him. Dad stuck his head in the door Wednesday night just after we closed. "All set for tomorrow?" he asked me. Mom heard him and came to the door.

"Come in and shut the door," she ordered. "What's this Maine business?"

"I thought the girls would like to see a lobster pound. You can buy the culls for next to nothing this time of year. The meat is just as good. You can have a lobster special next week."

"Where are you eating Thanksgiving dinner, Ed?" Mom wanted to know next.

"Well, I haven't given it much thought, Nettie."

"I think you have. Do you know what I think? I think you're sneaking up to see your mother and you're taking the girls along." Mom looked over to me to see if I was doing my homework at the counter. She lowered her voice.

"I might drop in for a minute to say hello. I haven't been home for a couple of years. Mother's getting along in years. She'd probably like to see Cleaver."

"I'm sure she would. Dogs are no problem for your mother. It's only people who cause her trouble. What about my girls? She's never wanted to see them. Or me," Mom said bitterly.

"You know how my mother is, Nettie," Dad replied. "She's set in her ways."

"Her ways are set in concrete, Ed. I don't want Sarah and Cori getting hurt by your mother. You better leave them here. Take Cleaver. He's crazy enough to get along with your mother. The girls and I will have Mama's turkey after I close up down here."

Dad whispered something I couldn't hear. Mom looked surprised.

"You're not lying to me, Ed? She said that?" Mom asked.

Dad lifted his right hand. "I swear that's what she said."

"It's all right, then," Mom told him. "It will be an experience for them. And take your car, for heaven's sake, not the Winnebago. You can leave Cleaver here this time."

"I need Cleaver," Dad said, "to break the ice, but I will take the car. I can put the lobsters in the trunk."

"No lobsters, please, unless you plan to cook and pick them. I don't have time to mess with them."

Cori and I had our backpacks ready when Dad picked us up early next morning. Cori sat in front and I sat in back with Cleaver, who kept his nose to the crack at the window, so it was cold in back. Every time I rolled the window shut, Cleaver put his left paw on my shoulder and whined. He had to have his smell wherever he went.

"How far is it to the lobster place?" Cori asked.

"It's pretty far," Dad said. "Put your seat back and take a nap."

"Where are we going to eat Thanksgiving dinner?" Cori asked next. "Are we going to have lobster or turkey?"

"How does turkey sound?"

"Okay, I guess. In a hotel or a restaurant?"

Dad didn't answer.

"Where, Dad?"

"Maybe in a house, Cori."

"Whose house?" When Cori was interested in something, she never let up.

"A house up in a town I know about."

Cori thought about that for a while. Then, "Who lives in the house, the person Mom said you should marry and go off to Florida with and leave her be?"

"Shut up, Cori," I said from the back. "Why don't you just wait and find out." Cleaver pulled his nose away from the window for a minute. He was curious about the conversation up front.

"There isn't any person I'm going off to Florida with, Cori. And I'm not going off to Florida."

"Mom said . . ."

"She was just talking, the way she does sometimes when she's upset. The place we're going to is called Castine."

"Where's Castine?" Cori persisted.

"It's up the coast of Maine. They have a lobster

pound there. It's on a harbor. In the summer they have lots of boats there."

"Come on, Dad. Tell me whose house."

"Your grandmother's."

You can bet that shut Cori up. Cleaver and I pricked up our ears. We had never seen Grandmother Stuart, even when Dad was living up on the hill with us. We'd heard Dad and Mom talking about her every once in a while. When they did, Mom always ended up mad and Dad would apologize and try to stop the discussion or else just walk away. Grandmother Stuart was a sore subject in the family.

I leaned forward to find out what was going on. There was no point in beating around the bush. "Are you going to leave us in the car, Dad? Mom says your mother doesn't want to see her or us. What about Cleaver? Does he get to see Grandmother Stuart?"

Cori had to say her piece. "Yeah, does she like dogs? Why doesn't she like children? What's wrong with us, anyway? Granny Rubin says we're the best kids anyone could have. We know how to behave if we want to."

"One thing at a time, Cori, one thing at a time. Your grandmother asked me to bring you up for Thanksgiving. I asked your mother. She said it was all right."

"How come she didn't ask Mom?" I demanded. "That's not fair, Dad. If we had known that, we wouldn't have come, would we, Cori?"

"No, indeed," said Cori. "Cleaver, either."

"I did ask your mother. I mean, my mother asked her. She said no, but she said you guys should go."

That was different. Maybe Mom would come the

69

next time. We had always wanted to see Grandmother Stuart. "How come she waited so long to have us come visit?" I asked.

"She didn't like it when I married your mother. She felt left out. First, she didn't like it at all when I quit school and helped Grandpa Rubin fix up the diner. She certainly didn't like it when I stayed on to marry your mother and went to work in the diner. She told me she was no longer interested in my life. It was nothing she approved of and she said it was nothing my father would have approved of if he had been alive. My parents had other plans for me."

We knew Dad's father had died a long time ago, but we didn't know anything about him. He was part of Dad's life that was never talked about. "What happened to your dad?" Cori asked.

"He died—he drowned, that is—in a sailing accident when I was in high school. He was a doctor. My mother and father believed I had to be a doctor, too, and work with my dad and take over his practice. My mother couldn't get used to Nettie and the diner."

Cori came right out and said it. "Was it because Mom's Jewish? Lots of people don't like Jews, Granny Rubin says."

Dad didn't answer for a long time. "Yeah," he said at last. "That's about it, Cori; most of it, anyway."

"Well, what about us? We're Jewish, too—half, anyway. Granny Rubin told me that," I said.

"You're both more like your mother than anyone else, that's for sure. But your grandmother still wants to see you, so that's where we're going. Better late than never."

"I don't want to go," Cori said. "I don't want to go at all. I'm not going in. Sarah can go if she wants, but not me. Cleaver and I will sit in the car. You two go eat turkey. Buy Cleaver and me a box of animal crackers."

Cori was right. Grandmother Stuart had no right to treat Mom and us the way she had and then decide she wanted to see us, as though we were some kind of curiosities. She could get angry with Dad for not being a doctor, he was her child, but the rest of us had nothing to do with that. "I'll stay in the car, too, Dad. I don't want to go where I'm not wanted. I'll stay with Cori. You take Cleaver."

Dad pulled the Toyota over to the side of the highway. "Look," he said, "I can't promise you anything. I have spent the last twenty years fighting or running away from my mother. She's getting old and lonely and I reckon she's changing her ways. I'm asking you to come along. If you don't want to, we'll go back home. Let me promise you something. If you guys come along and anything goes wrong, one snooty look or one bad remark—anything like that—we'll leave and that will be that. Grandmother Stuart isn't mean or wicked, she's just confused in what she thinks. Let's give her a chance. You'll like the house. It's almost on the water. It's a big house, a really big white house."

"Is she rich?" Cori wanted to know next.

"I guess you could call her rich," Dad answered. "And she has a dog."

71

"A dog!" Cori shouted. "Oh, boy, a dog for Cleaver to play with. What kind of a dog?"

"What kind do you think, Cori?"

"A Bernese mountain dog?"

"Yes," Dad said. "A genuine Bernese mountain dog. Her name is Crista."

14

It *was* a big house, a big, old, white house set back on a big front yard across the street from the water. A white fence went all around the yard. A brick walk went up from the street to a black door. Dad banged twice with the brass whale knocker. We could hear the echo deep inside, then a bark and some steps. The black door opened and a dog bounded out, a dog just like Cleaver, but not so big.

Cleaver was hanging around in back of Cori, who held his leash. When he saw Crista, his tail stiffened. Crista's tail stiffened. She looked at Cleaver, who stuck close to Cori. Then he wagged his bushy big tail. Crista wagged her tail and the two Bernese mountain dogs got down to some serious sniffing.

Cori and I were watching the dogs and hardly heard an elegant voice say, "I think they're going to be friends, don't you? Why don't we all go inside and introduce ourselves?"

The warm smell of turkey filled the hallway. Cleaver lost interest in Crista and put his nose up to sniff. He liked to know where good smells were coming from.

"I think your dog is more interested in the turkey than he is in his sister," Grandmother Stuart said.

"You mean Crista is Cleaver's sister?" Cori asked.

"Of course. Didn't Edward—your father, I mean—tell you?"

"No," Cori said softly. She bent down to scratch Crista under the chin, which was what Cleaver liked. "Why didn't you tell us, Dad?"

I knew, but I didn't say anything. Dad pretended to be embarrassed and said he must have forgotten. It was just as well. If Mom had known that Dad gave his mother Cleaver's sister at the same time he gave us Cleaver, we never would have had a dog.

His mother knew, too. "Oh, dear," she said in her friendly, firm voice. "I'll go see how the bird is coming along. Take Sarah and Corinthia up to their rooms, Edward."

Cori and I had two large rooms at the front of the house, where we could see the harbor. There was a bathroom in between the rooms just for us. Both the rooms had wallpaper like old quilts, and furniture like in the antique shop in Stanhope we went in once. Over Cori's bed was a silky white canopy. Dad said my room used to be his. When he went off, his mother had it redone.

"She is really rich, isn't she, Sarah?" Cori said when Dad had left.

"It sure looks that way, doesn't it?"

"Do you suppose if she likes us, we can come up and visit in the summer? Boy, would Cleaver love to go swimming in that water."

We were looking out at the harbor when Dad came back in and asked us how we were getting along. We said fine. Cori asked Dad to ask his mother not to call her Corinthia.

"I think you'd better tell her yourself, Cori. I think she likes the name. She said it had a good sound."

"She did?"

"Yes," Dad said. "She said Sarah was a fine, solid name and Corinthia had a good sound. She said you looked like a Corinthia."

I groaned inside. Just like always, Cori was getting the attention because she had a fancy name, one that she didn't even like. I was left with a fine, solid name. That meant I was a fine, solid girl, somebody people could count on. I wished Granny Rubin had gotten to the hospital early with one of her fancy names when I was born.

Grandmother Stuart called up the steps to say the turkey was on the table. Dad told us she said grace and we should bow our heads for a minute before we started in on our fruit cocktail.

It turned out Grandmother Stuart didn't say grace. She asked Dad to. He asked the Lord to bless our food and we started eating. Cleaver sat politely beside my chair and pretended he wasn't interested in the food but he would do me a favor and eat anything I gave him. I didn't see Crista anywhere. Cleaver got a hard look from Grandmother Stuart, but she didn't say anything. I figured dogs ate in the kitchen in her house or maybe there was a dog room we hadn't seen yet out in back.

When we finished, Grandmother Stuart announced she would take us for a walk around the harbor before it was altogether dark. Dad would clean up. "That was your father's job when he was growing up, cleaning up after supper," she told us. "Bring your dog and I'll fetch Crista. They don't need leashes this time of year. Crista will show Cleaver the way."

It was cold outside, so cold that you could see your breath. Dad hadn't told us to bring our heavy jackets, and we were shivering inside our light school jackets. Grandmother Stuart didn't seem to notice. She kept talking about how she and Dad always took a walk after supper to check on the boats, which ones had berthed during the day and which ones had gone out. "The family had a boat once, a sailboat. Your grandfather took it out one afternoon," she told us. "A sudden squall came up and it capsized. He was too proud to wear a life jacket, because he was such a powerful swimmer. He must have hit his head. I have always blamed myself for not being with him."

"Why?" asked Cori. She could say the dumbest things sometimes.

"Why, I could have saved him or . . ." She paused. "I could have drowned with him."

Cori thought about that for a minute. "Then Dad wouldn't have had a mother and we wouldn't have had you for a grandmother."

That hadn't occurred to Grandmother Stuart, I guess. "You're right, Corinthia. You're absolutely right. I was being a silly old woman, feeling sorry for myself. We better go back now. It's getting chilly." She put an arm around each of us and called to Crista to bring Cleaver back. They had run ahead and Cleaver must have decided to go swimming. He ran toward us shaking himself and wagging his tail. Next to eating and sniffing, he liked swimming best.

We slept late the next morning. When we came down for breakfast, there was an expensive new down jacket on Cori's chair and one on mine.

"We have heavy jackets, ma'am," I explained. "We forgot to bring them."

"You didn't forget. Your father didn't tell you you would need them. If you don't want them at home you can leave them here for the next time you come to visit. And stop calling me 'ma'am,' please. What do you call your other grandmother?"

"Granny Rubin," Cori said. "She's always been Granny Rubin."

"Then I might as well be Granny Stuart. That suits me. How does it suit you?"

We nodded and went to work on our French toast. Cori didn't say anything about not wanting to be a Corinthia. She must have decided she could be a Cori in the diner and a Corinthia in the big white house.

I noticed someone was missing. "Where's Cleaver?" I asked.

"Your father took them both downtown. I always take Crista for a walk in the morning, but I let Edward do it today. I wanted to talk to you both."

That sounded serious. We were getting along pretty well with Granny Stuart, and I wasn't sure we were ready for serious talk. Cori and I put our heads down over the French toast and waited.

"There is no fool like an old fool, they say," Granny Stuart began, "and I am not going to be an old fool. I was a middle-aged fool and your grandfather was, too, may he rest in peace. We expected your father to grow up and be like us. We thought he had an obligation to his parents for some reason. When your grandfather died I thought Edward had a double obligation, to look after me the way his father had and to be just like his father.

"He tried—I didn't realize it at the time, but he tried, he tried very hard. But it wasn't what he wanted and he couldn't do it. I thought he left school to hurt me, when in fact he flunked out to escape me. I figured that out later. He married your mother and I wouldn't forgive him. I loved him, so I blamed your mother. That was wicked of me. Do you understand?"

We nodded, and she went on. "Your mother and her family weren't like us. I resented that, too. I refused to meet her and I didn't want to have anything to do with my grandchildren. I sat up here in this big white house with my bitter memories.

"When your mother and father separated, I was

happy because I thought perhaps Edward would come back here to be with me. But he didn't. All he did was give me a dog." Granny Stuart laughed. "Your mother and I both got a dog."

"Cleaver made a difference when Dad left," I said. "He made a lot of difference."

"Well, Crista made a difference in my life, too. The house wasn't quite so empty. She was someone to talk to. The more I talked to Crista, the more I realized I had been very foolish for twenty years or more and it was time for me to change. I asked Edward to bring your mother and you up here. Now that you are here, I understand how very much I have lost out on. I hope you will come visit whenever you can. I hope your mother will forgive me and come with you and bring Granny Rubin along. I want to tell them I am sorry. Will you help me do that?"

"Gee," Cori said, "that would be great. Two grand-mothers, that would be really great. We wouldn't need a grandfather, would we, Sarah?"

"One last thing before I shut up and have a good cry," Granny Stuart said. "Sometimes I think it's mostly my fault your father went off from his family last year. I must have made him feel guilty. Maybe he was trying to punish me by wrecking his own life. We had a long talk last night. I told him he has an obligation to you and Benedicta. He doesn't have any to me. He loves you all, you know. He made a mistake—maybe we'll never understand why—and he wants to be together with you. It won't happen again."

"He told us that, too," I said. "It's Mom. He left her

without giving her a chance, she says. Mom has a lot of pride. She says she can do without him."

"I understand that, Sarah. Can you tell her for me that my pride never did me any good? You can't eat it. Try to make her see how much your dad loves her."

"We'll talk to her, but it probably won't do any good. Granny Rubin keeps telling her the same thing. Mom's pretty stubborn when she wants to be."

"Let's keep our fingers crossed. Why don't you put on your new jackets to see if they fit and go look for your father and the dogs down by the harbor. I'm going to have my cry and another cup of tea."

15

Mom didn't say much when Dad brought us home Friday night. Linda had left early to go to the movies with Mark. We helped clean up and then sat around in the back booth to tell Mom and Granny Rubin about the big white house and Christa and how nice Granny Stuart was. All Mom said was that she was glad we had a nice visit and we didn't need new down jackets. Our old heavy jackets were good enough.

Granny Rubin said it was good to have a new grandmother, you could never have too many. She was interested in how Cleaver got along with his sister. When we told her he didn't seem to care one way or another, she nodded her head. Cleaver was too young for girls, she said, even if they were his sister. When she heard he went swimming in the cold water, she cackled with laughter. "See, Benedicta, I told you Cleaver was crazy.

Going swimming on Thanksgiving, who ever heard of such a thing?"

Cleaver heard his name and came out from behind the counter to see what was going on. Granny Rubin gave him a little piece of cake. "He knows his name, Benedicta. That's something at least. What do you suppose he's going to learn next?"

Mom wasn't listening. She was sitting there with a faraway look in her eyes. "Oh," she said suddenly, "I almost forgot, Cori. Margo Michaels is giving a sleep-over tomorrow night. I told Mrs. Michaels you'd be there. Did I do right?"

"A sleep-over! Oh, boy!" Cori shouted. "I have to go up to the house right away and get packed. Oh, boy, oh, boy, oh, boy! Did you hear, Sarah, a sleep-over?"

"I heard, Cori. What's so special about a sleep-over? It's just down the road at the Michaelses'."

"Calm down, Cori," Mom said. "It's not until six o'clock tomorrow. Mrs. Michaels is buying pizza. All you have to take are your pajamas and a sleeping bag."

"Who else is going, Mom? Did Mrs. Michaels say? I hope it's not that awful Terry. What about Sandra? Is she going?"

Mom explained that Mrs. Michaels had not said who else was going to the sleep-over. Cori could talk to Margo in the morning and find out. Now she had to go to bed. We walked up the hill with Granny Rubin.

The sleep-over was all Cori talked about on Saturday. It was the first one she had been invited to. We weren't asked to too many birthday parties and sleep-overs. Cori spent most of the morning on the phone with Margo. Terry Watts was invited, along with Sue Montgomery and Carol Poquette.

"Terry's not so bad," I reassured Cori. "She just talks a lot."

"She thinks she's better than everybody else," Cori said. "She doesn't speak to half the kids in her class. She says she's richer than the rest of us. She's always talking about what her parents gave her or where she went on vacation."

"She probably is richer," I said. "Mom says her father owns the mall and the hotel. You have to be friendly with everyone, Cori, or you won't be invited to any more sleep-overs."

Margo lived on the other side of the rest home. Cleaver and I walked Cori down. Margo and Sue and Carol came to the door squealing with excitement. Mrs. Michaels said she would send Cori home in the middle of the morning. Cori hugged Cleaver and we walked back to the Good Luck. It was cold and dark along the road. I felt lonely. When you thought about it, Cori and I *were* different, or we seemed different. Other kids did things we didn't do. Most of them had things we didn't have. I remembered Granny Stuart and her big house. It would be nice to go visit in Castine—not just to have something to talk about like the other kids, maybe, but to be somewhere for a while where you didn't have to clean up and work on Sundays. Maybe I could take Helen Yeng with me. Maybe Mom and Dad would make up. It was about time something really good happened.

It was a busy night at the diner. You could never tell about Saturday nights. Sometimes nobody came by after seven. Other times we were packed right up to closing time. This Saturday night other people must have been cold and lonely, too. They needed some lights and company. I told Mom if she put in a jukebox we'd have a lot more business from high-school kids. She said she had enough noise in her life for the time being.

We were late in getting to bed. I had scarcely gone to sleep when Granny Rubin woke me up. "Sarah," she whispered so as not to wake up Mom, "that crazy Cleaver won't come in. He wanted to go out and now he won't come in. I'm too old to go chasing that crazy dog in the dark."

I stuffed my feet into my sneakers and threw on my bathrobe. I stumbled downstairs and out the back door. I hollered for Cleaver. "Let's leave the outside light on. He'll be back in a little while," I told Granny Rubin. "Maybe he went out to the barn. You go to bed, Granny Rubin."

"That's a crazy dog, that Cleaver. First he was in the kitchen. Then he was up in Cori's room. Then he came to my room. Then he went back to the kitchen and scratched at the door. He doesn't know what he wants."

The phone rang. I grabbed it before Mom could hear it. It was Mrs. Michaels. Cleaver had shown up at their house and wanted in. She let him in. He headed straight upstairs to where the girls were pretending to be asleep. He said hello to all of them and flopped down in the corner. He was a nice dog, Mrs. Michaels said, and he might as well spend the night. The girls wanted him. Anyway, it was too cold for me to walk down the road and get him.

Granny Rubin and I went back to bed. At three-thirty someone was pounding on the back door. Mom heard it first. She was unlocking the door when I came down. Cori and Cleaver and Mr. Michaels, in a jacket over his bathrobe, were waiting outside. Cleaver was wagging his tail. Cori was crying. Mr. Michaels was looking embarrassed.

"Cori wanted to bring Cleaver home," he apologized. "I guess he was being a nuisance and keeping the girls awake. He wouldn't sleep in the kitchen and he wouldn't leave without Cori. It didn't matter to Margo's mother and me, but one of the girls got upset. Anyway, I'm sorry to bother you at this hour of the night."

"We're the ones who should be sorry, Mr. Michaels," Mom said. "I didn't know he was down there or I would have come to bring him home. Why didn't you tell me, Sarah?"

"It's all right, Mrs. Stuart. We told Cori she could have her sleep-over tomorrow night, just with Margo, if that's all right with you. She can go to school Monday morning with Margo on the bus. We'll be sure they get to bed early. It's not the dog's fault. He was looking after Cori. We'll see you tomorrow night, Cori. Don't worry about it." He smiled at Cori and scratched Cleaver's ears.

"It was that awful Terry Watts," Cori howled as soon as Mr. Michaels had left. "Cleaver didn't do anything. He was being friendly. We were telling ghost stories and being real quiet. Cleaver was sleeping in the corner. When we finished we all said good-night, all of us except Terry, to Cleaver. He came over to kiss us good-night. Terry started to yell and scream that Cleaver was trying to bite her. She said she wasn't going to stay in the same room with a dirty old dog. She wouldn't shut up. Mrs. Michaels had to come in."

"Cleaver had no business at the sleep-over, Cori. He wasn't invited. I wish Sarah and Granny Rubin had told me where he was. I would have brought him home."

"You need your sleep, Benedicta. Sarah and I can look after things," Granny Rubin said. "You heard what the man said. It wasn't Cleaver's fault. It was that Terry Watts girl, the one who doesn't like our Corinthia. She was the one who caused the trouble. Cleaver's a good dog. He knows his manners."

Cori started to cry again. "That Terry. I hate her. You know what she said, Mom? She said she and Sue Montgomery were Margo's best friends. She said I only got invited to the sleep-over because Margo's mother made her. She said I didn't belong in their sleep-over club. She wasn't really scared of Cleaver. She only did it to get at me."

Mom held Cori close and let her cry. "I don't know why, Cori," she said, "but girls are awfully mean sometimes. For all you know, you and Terry Watts may be best friends this time next week. Do you remember, Mama, when I was in the fourth grade, I had a different best friend every other day? I was jealous about all of them. You, too, Sarah. You always felt left out if you didn't have someone special."

"Well, it's true, Mom. I don't have any friends now except Helen."

"That's not so, Mom." Cori stopped crying. "Sarah's the most popular girl in her room. Everybody knows that. She'll be captain of the field-hockey team next year. She just likes Helen best and doesn't want anybody else. That's what it is."

"What about you, Cori?" Granny Rubin asked. "Is crazy Cleaver your only good friend? How come you're going to have a sleep-over at Margo's tomorrow night? How come I'm losing my baby two nights in a row if she's so unpopular?"

"Margo said I was to come back tomorrow night when the other girls weren't there," Cori told us proudly. "Just before Cleaver and I left, she came down to ask if I could come back. She told her mother I was her best friend. She said Terry Watts was a stuck-up pig."

Mom sighed and shook her head. "Girls," she said. "Give me boys anytime."

"You want a boy?" Granny Rubin asked. "I'll get you a boy, Benedicta, a big boy with curly hair and blue eyes, named Ed. He can be your best friend."

This time Mom didn't snap at Granny Rubin. She sighed again and took Cori's hand to take her up to bed.

16

On the day before Christmas vacation started, they handed out report cards. Mine weren't ever very good, especially after Dad left, but Mom seemed to understand. She never scolded me. "They'll get better, Sarah," she used to say. "When you go to high school I bet you'll be a straight-A student. People develop at different speeds. I didn't have many A's in high school, but I did very well in college."

Granny Rubin agreed. "That's true, Sarah. Your mother almost made Phi Beta Kappa. So you see, Sarah, you have the brains. You'll have to learn to use them." Granny Rubin took more interest in my report card than Mom did.

When the last bell rang and I was gathering up my books, Mrs. Porter, my English teacher, asked me to come see her for a few minutes.

She closed the door to the teachers' room and sat down at the table. She told me to sit next to her. Mrs. Porter was strict, fair but strict. I worked pretty hard for her in English class, harder than I did in any of my other courses, even though my grade didn't show it. I wished I had packed my bag a little quicker and left before Mrs. Porter trapped me.

She reached in her briefcase and pulled out a batch of compositions—mine. When she handed back your compositions you were supposed to think about the comments she made at the end and write underneath whether you agreed with them or not. Most of the kids scribbled "yes" and handed them back. Mom and Granny Rubin would read her comments. Mom usually said, "Well, Sarah, she's gone to a lot of trouble here. You might as well tell her what you think."

So I wrote a couple of sentences to tell Mrs. Porter what I was trying to say, although I hadn't said it very well. The best composition I wrote was about Cleaver and the skunk. Mrs. Porter wrote "SUPER" in big letters, and underneath, "Now I know you can write." The other compositions, which were supposed to be about something you read or some topic assigned by Mrs. Porter, I didn't do so well on.

"I'm sorry I couldn't give you a really good grade, Sarah. Most of your work in English is about average. You don't do well on the tests."

I nodded. There wasn't much I could say to that. Tests didn't give me room to answer. I often got confused about what Mrs. Porter wanted. By the time I had it figured out, the bell would ring

"On the other hand," Mrs. Porter said with a friendly smile, "on the other hand, some of your compositions are really great. The one about your dog made me laugh for a long time." She shuffled the papers around and pulled out the one about Cleaver and the skunk. She read the first part to herself. She was laughing when she put it down. "What kind of a dog is this Cleaver?"

"He's a Bernese mountain dog. My dad says they're very special dogs. They're field dogs, water dogs, sheep dogs, cart dogs, and house dogs all rolled up in one. He's just a dog, really, but he's one of the family."

"Does he get into a lot of trouble, or do you make some of it up?" Mrs. Porter wanted to know. She had seen his picture in the paper when he scared off the robber.

"I don't think so. It just seems that way. He's always hanging around waiting to be fed or loved, so we pay more attention to him than we should." I went on to tell her about Cleaver at Cori's sleep-over. "You see, Mrs. Porter, it wasn't Cleaver's fault. He stays closest to Cori because she's the baby. All he wanted was to be friendly to her friends."

"Your parents are divorced?" she asked next.

"They've been separated for over a year now. Maybe they're going to get back together. Dad wants to, but Mom isn't so sure."

"She runs the diner all by herself?"

"She runs the kitchen. There's Mrs. Muldowney at the counter in the morning and Linda Kowelski from twelve o'clock on. My sister and I help out in the afternoons and evenings."

"Does that keep you from your schoolwork?" Mrs. Porter asked.

"Sometimes, when we're busy until eight-thirty or nine, but that's not very often. I have enough time." There was no point in blaming Mom for my grades. She was probably already blaming herself.

"But your grades aren't so good, are they?" Mrs. Porter persisted.

The way she kept on with questions made me nervous. What did she want? She already knew my grades weren't so hot. They were only good enough to keep me passing up to the next grade every year. They weren't any worse than lots of other kids' grades. Why the sudden interest in mine?

"Would you like to do something special for me for the rest of the school year?" Mrs. Porter now asked.

I was really confused. I had just told her I didn't have all that much free time. I mumbled something about how I guessed I would.

"The thing is, Sarah, I have a feeling you are a writer, someone might say a born writer. It's the way you see what goes on and the way you think about it and then the way you write about it. I don't say it's always good, but it's always different. You have your own, distinctive way of dealing with what goes on around you."

That sounded good, but I couldn't take the credit for being distinctive. There was the diner, there were

Granny Rubin and Mom and Cori, all of whom were a little bit odd; and there was Cleaver, too. When you looked at it, they were what was special. I tried to explain that to Mrs. Porter.

"You're right, Sarah, but you are the one who sees that and you are the one who knows how it is different in a way from how other kids are growing up. Your best friend is Helen Yeng, isn't she, not some of the other girls? Why do you suppose that is?"

"I suppose it's because she's Chinese and because she has to work, too. Her grades are a lot better than mine, I can tell you. She makes straight A's."

"I'm sure she does, but she doesn't write about herself and her family the way you do, and probably never will. It's too bad. She has a lot to say, as much as you do, Sarah, perhaps."

"Are you a writer, Mrs. Porter?" I wasn't sure exactly what a writer was, since I wasn't much of a reader.

She laughed. "I used to think I was when I was at college. I wrote some poems, which were printed in the student literary magazine. If I were to look at them now, I'd die of embarrassment. No, I'm not a writer. I'm a good reader and I know writing when I see it. I can tell you, Sarah, you write better—maybe I should say, more distinctively—than anyone I've read since I've been a teacher. That is fifteen years. Now, may I tell you what I want you to do?"

"Yes, ma'am," I said. I was puzzled over what was going on.

"I want you to keep a journal—not a diary, mind

you, but a journal. Write in it when something happens you want to remember or when you think of something that pleases you. Later on, I'd like you to write some things for me like the Cleaver-and-the-skunk story, or something more personal if you're willing to share it with me. Write about things that are important to you. After a while you'll be tempted to make things up. That's usually when young people start to go wrong. Until you are older and more secure, deal with what you are familiar with. Will you do that for me, Sarah? You have something special, I'm sure of it, and it would be a great pity to lose it.

"Well," she went on, "I have to go over to the mall and do my Christmas shopping. I hope you have a good Christmas and I hope things work out for your family. You need a dad as well as a dog in your life."

Mom looked at my report card. "Hmm, it's about the same as usual, isn't it? Someday you're going to surprise me, Sarah."

I was bursting with pride. I had missed the bus and walked home thinking about nothing but what Mrs. Porter had said. "Mom," I said, "I had a long talk with my English teacher, Mrs. Porter. Do you know what she said, Mom? She said I was very special. She said I was the best writer she ever had. She didn't exactly say so, but she thinks I can be a real writer. And she wants me to keep a journal. She liked what I wrote about Cleaver and the skunk. I see things in a distinctive way, she says, and I live in a distinctive family. You see, Mom, I'm not as dumb as you think."

94

"You've always been distinctive to me, Sarah, since before you were born. First children are always special. Most of them grow up thinking they are special, too, but most of them probably aren't. They are just the first ones to come along. Now you *know* you are special, at least to Mrs. Porter as well as to your dad and Granny Rubin and me and Cori and Cleaver here. Even if you weren't, I'd love you just as much."

It was Cleaver's ice-cream time. Linda was busy with her homework, so Mom got up to serve him. "And I never said you were dumb, Sarah. That was your idea, not mine." She gave Cleaver an extra scoop and rubbed his big head fondly. "Oh, Cleaver," she said. "You're changing all of us. You're a regular big sweet potato, Cleaver."

17

For Christmas Granny Rubin gave me a neat leather-bound journal. "For Sarah the Writer," she wrote on the Santa Claus card tucked inside. Mom gave me an expensive silver ball-point pen to go with the journal. Dad left three square packages, one big and two not so big, under the tree. When Mom wasn't around, he had made Cleaver sit on the front steps of the Good Luck Diner and Deli and taken his picture. He gave Cori and me each a picture for our bureaus. The big one was for Mom. The card on it said, "Please put my picture over the cash register. Cleaver the Watchdog."

Mom laughed and showed Cleaver his picture. He didn't recognize himself and went back to sleep beside the Christmas tree. When Granny Rubin asked Mom if she intended to hang the picture in the diner, she said she'd have to think about it. "Well, that's something, anyway," Granny Rubin grumbled.

Christmas was on a Thursday and Mom closed the diner for a long weekend. "Everyone else is taking off," she said. "We might as well do the same." Her friend from college days, Meredith, had married a guy who owned a ski lodge and tow in Stowe, Vermont, and once a year we visited for a long weekend.

I tied our skis to the roof rack of the station wagon. Cori carried our boots and jackets out and put them in the back. She left the rear door of the wagon up while she went inside for our suitcase. While Mom was inside giving Granny Rubin last-minute instructions, Cleaver slipped out the back door and jumped into the back of the station wagon.

Cleaver always knew when we were going off, even before we ourselves knew, and insisted on going along. Mom said he was clairvoyant. I think it was because he took notice of what was going on around him; when we didn't do what we usually did, he started to worry.

"Get out this minute," Mom ordered when she discovered where he was. Cleaver put his head down between his paws and looked upset.

"Out, Cleaver!" Cori and I shouted. Cleaver looked more worried and whined a little to tell us how he felt.

"This is too much," Mom said angrily. She reached in and grabbed Cleaver's collar. He rolled over on his back and whined some more. Then he cried a little bit to let us know he was really upset. Mom couldn't budge him.

Granny Rubin came out. She reached in and patted Cleaver, who licked her hand. "He wants to go, too, Benedicta."

"Of course he wants to go, Mama. He wants to go anywhere he can be a nuisance."

"He wasn't a nuisance at Granny Stuart's," Cori said. "He was very good, wasn't he, Sarah?"

I didn't answer. It would be sort of nice to have a real vacation without having to look after a dog you had to look after every other day of the year.

"Cleaver needs a vacation, too, Benedicta. I'll get his leash." We had given him a new red leash for Christmas, almost twice as long as his old one. Granny Rubin hustled into the house.

"What is Meredith going to think when we show up with this hulk?" Mom asked no one in particular.

"You can tell her he's a mountain dog," Cori said. "I bet you they don't have any of them up in Stowe."

Mom looked at me. "Let's have a vote. I say no. Cori says yes. Granny can't vote because she's not going. What do you say?"

I looked at Mom. She was tossing the car keys in her hand, anxious to get going on her three-day vacation. I looked at Cori, who was in back with her arms around Cleaver. Whether we took Cleaver or not, Mom was going to spend all her time talking to Meredith about the good old days. He was a pest sometimes, but he was part of the family, too. "I don't know," I said. "He's pretty good most of the time. He'll sleep in the car if he has to. He sleeps in the Winnebago at night, on the front seat. We better take him. Otherwise, he'll make life miserable for Granny Rubin."

"Sarah's right," Granny Rubin said. "I need a vacation, too. I'll be all right, Benedicta. Go on, go. Enjoy." She hugged Mom and winked at Cleaver.

Cleaver put his head on Cori's lap to tell her he'd be a good dog. Mom slammed her door shut. She spun down the driveway. "Your seat belt, Mom," I said. She slammed on the brakes and snapped on her seat belt. Then she looked straight ahead for a minute, without speaking, hands on the wheel. Then she put her arm around me. "You're a softy, Sarah," she said.

Cori and I were pretty good skiers. On Sundays Mom sometimes took us to the tow in Hartfield. She skied with us there, but up in Stowe she curled up in front of the fire and she and Meredith reviewed the story of their lives. Meredith and Gus, her husband, didn't have any kids. Gus looked after us when he wasn't busy. He told us it had snowed a lot two days before Christmas and the lodge was full. "They'll be sleeping in the dining room by dark. Five or six weekends like this and we'll make the season."

Gus made friends with Cleaver right away. "This sure is some dog," he said. "Look at his paws. He has webbing between his toes so he can walk in the snow."

The webbing didn't do Cleaver much good at first. As soon as he hit the snow, he fell through up to his belly. He looked at Cori and Gus and me to find out what he should do. Cori said, "I guess he doesn't know he's a snow dog yet. Come on, Cleaver, get over here on the path."

Cleaver struggled over to the path from the lodge to the big barn. Out beyond, the lift was pulling people up the side of the mountain. The sun was just peeping over the top. Cori and I snapped on our skis and headed for the lift. Gus joined us. "We'll have a run or two before it gets too crowded. You two go on up first. I'll hold your dog."

"I don't know, Gus," I said. "We better put him inside. He's pretty strong. He likes to go wherever we go."

"Don't worry," Gus said. He doubled up Cleaver's leash. "I'll hold him tight. Cleaver and I are good friends, eh, Cleaver?" He scratched Cleaver in back of his ears. Cleaver wagged his tail and sat down to watch. Gus knelt beside him.

Cori and I only went to the top of the first lift. The really good skiers switched over to the other lift and went on up to the top. We looked down to the bottom of the slope. Gus and Cleaver were waiting patiently.

I pushed off first. Cori, who was watching, told me Cleaver pushed off at the same time, leaving Gus sitting on the snow with a surprised look on his face, shouting at Cleaver to come back, dogs weren't allowed on the slopes.

I was halfway down when I saw Cleaver charging up the hill as fast as he could. I turned a little to slip by and Cleaver turned a little to meet me and we both ended up on our backs. Cleaver got up first and stood over me licking my face. I tried to get up, too, but my ankle gave way beneath me. I unsnapped my skis and tried again. It was no good. My ankle really hurt. Cleaver was upset. He barked down the hill at Gus, then ran halfway down the slope and back again.

When Gus saw that something was wrong, he and Cori came to help. Cori took Cleaver's leash, and Gus helped me down to the lodge. He moved my foot back and forth to see where it hurt. "I don't think it's broken," he told Mom. "I'll take her in to the doctor's to be sure." He took some crutches out of the closet and helped me to the Jeep.

"It's only a bad sprain," the doctor told me. "You're lucky it's not worse. What happened?"

I told him about the collision with Cleaver. The doctor laughed. "You probably fell on your dog. That's what saved you. I'll wrap it for you. Stay off it as much as you can. You'll be all right in a week."

Mom wasn't very sympathetic. "Well, Sarah, you voted to bring the dog along. If it were worse, I wouldn't say it serves you right, but since it's only a sprain, I will say it just once. It serves you right. Cleaver should have stayed at home."

I sat by the fire for the rest of Saturday listening to Meredith and Mom talk about the diner and Ed and the lodge and Gus and Cori and me and Granny Rubin and Meredith's niece, who'd won a scholarship to Harvard, and Gus's folks, who came up from Florida every spring and stayed too long. Sunday morning I took my journal and hobbled to the kitchen table. I began writing about Cleaver's vacation in Stowe, Vermont. It was better than listening to Mom and Meredith.

Gus took Cori and Cleaver cross-country skiing. He said Cleaver thumped along behind them on his webbed feet the way he was supposed to. "He's a snow dog, you can tell that," Gus said. "Once he puts his mind to something, he's about as smart as any dog I've ever seen. I wonder what got into him yesterday out there on the slope."

Mom made a nasty remark. "He's a watchdog, too, Gus. He watches for a chance to make trouble, don't you, Cleaver?"

Cleaver was snoozing in front of the fire. He didn't hear what Mom said. He was all worn out from being a snow dog.

18

Mom said I had to be careful with my ankle; otherwise I wouldn't be able to go back to school after vacation. The holidays were an easy time at the diner. They didn't need me. Cori grumbled about having to do my work, so Mom let her spell Granny Rubin at the register every once in a while. She shut up after that. When she came up to the house at night she had to tell me about ten times how much money she had collected.

There wasn't anything to do at the house. Granny Rubin stayed with me in the mornings, and Cleaver was there in the afternoons. After his trips to Granny Stuart's and Stowe, Cleaver decided to be a house dog as well as a diner dog, at least until it was ice-cream time. Then I had to hobble to the door to let him out. He tore down the hill, ears flapping, and let everyone there know what time it was.

I went back to work on my journal. I finished my account of how Cleaver and I ran into each other on the slope. When I read it over, parts of it out loud to Cleaver, who wasn't much interested, it didn't seem to be the way I wanted it to be. Mom read it and said, "It's very good, Sarah, but I think you have to make Cleaver into more of a character. In what you have written he seems like a friendly, dumb dog. That's not how he is, and it certainly isn't how we talk about him. He's a member of the family. He has his own personality like the rest of us. You should try to bring that out more. Ask yourself, Where would we be without Cleaver?"

I was still sort of mad about what had happened on the slope and losing half my vacation. "We could do without him, Mom. We could do without him just fine. We did all right before he came. Sometimes he's more trouble than he's worth."

Mom thought about that. "Maybe you're right, Sarah. He is a pest, that's for sure. I must be getting softheaded in my old age to put up with him."

Then she went down the hill. I thought about what I had said. It didn't make me feel very good. I couldn't see us without Cleaver. He had held us together in the months after Dad left. I sat at the kitchen table and rewrote the account of the accident. I made it more my fault than Cleaver's. If I hadn't swerved, he wouldn't have run into me. I put down how upset he was afterward and how he ran down the slope to get help. I liked it better when I read it over.

By Wednesday night I was able to hop around pretty well. That night Mom told us she was going off on New Year's Day, when the diner was closed, and might not be back until late at night.

"Where are you going, Mom?" Cori asked. "Can I go?"

"I can't tell you and you can't go."

That wasn't like Mom. She didn't keep things from us. It must have been pretty important. Cori wouldn't let up. "Why can't you tell us? Are you going off with Dad somewhere?"

"I'm certainly not going off with your father and I'm not going to answer any more questions. Granny Rubin is in charge. I don't want you to cause her any trouble. You won't have to worry about Cleaver. I'm taking him with me."

That didn't sound right. Mom wasn't hot on taking Cleaver with her in the car, no matter how much he wanted to go. She said he slobbered all over the windows so she couldn't see out the back. All he did was complain about being left in the car when she went into a store. As far as she was concerned, Cleaver was not a car dog.

"How come you're taking Cleaver and not me?" Cori wanted to know. "You don't like to take him places."

"Well, I'm taking him this time and I'm leaving early in the morning. Don't wait up tomorrow night. The roads may be bad."

Cori made a last effort to trap her. "Roads to where, Mom?"

Mom didn't answer. She took us each by the hand and we went up to bed.

She was gone the next morning when we woke up. We went downstairs and asked Granny Rubin where she went. "She didn't say and I didn't ask. If she didn't tell you, she wasn't going to tell me. I'm only her mother."

"But she took Cleaver," Cori protested.

"Good for her. We'll have a peaceful day. Maybe she's going off to find him a new home. He's getting too big for the diner."

Cori looked at Granny Rubin to see if she was teasing. She looked pretty serious. Tears ran down Cori's face. "She couldn't do that. She wouldn't dare do that. We all love Cleaver."

Granny Rubin pulled Cori into her lap. She wiped her tears on her apron and gave her a sip of coffee. "I was only teasing you, child. I don't know why she took the big lummox. We'll have to get along without him if we can."

Most of the morning I kept thinking about Mom and Cleaver. Cori had her nose in the television set. Granny Rubin was making a cake. I kept remembering what I had said about Cleaver a couple of days before. Had Mom taken me seriously and found another home for Cleaver? She wouldn't have told us that's what she was doing until afterward. I felt sick.

When Cori came in my room I had to tell her what I had said to Mom and what she had said.

Cori started to sob, not loud enough for Granny

Rubin to hear, but long, throbbing sobs. She ran into her room. "That's what she did," Cori moaned. "And Granny Rubin knows it, too. That's why she's making us a cake. And you, Sarah, you knew it, too, and you didn't stop her. You let her think it was all right, that we didn't want Cleaver around. He was my dog, too. He slept in my room, not yours. You were jealous, weren't you? Oh, oh, I hate you, Sarah." She threw herself onto her bed and pulled the sheet over her face. "Get out of my room, Sarah. Don't ever come in here again."

There was no point in trying to explain to Cori how it was. She didn't talk to anyone the rest of the day. She stayed in her room with the door closed. Granny Rubin stuck her head in to see if she was coming down with a bug. When she didn't get an answer, she asked me what was wrong with Corinthia. I shrugged my shoulders. It was too complicated to explain.

The house seemed empty without Cleaver. I moped around, limping more than I had to so Granny Rubin would feel sorry for me. I tried to write in my journal, but I couldn't. I read what I had written the second time. Now that didn't seem right, either. I scratched a big X across the pages.

After supper I started looking out the window for Mom's headlights. "She told us she would be late, Sarah," Granny Rubin said. "There's no point in looking for her now."

"But where did she go, Granny Rubin? You must

know. It's not like Mom to go off without telling us where she's going."

"I don't ask your mother questions about her life. That is her business. She's a grown woman," Granny sniffed. "It *is* strange, though. I don't remember that she ever did anything like this before."

At ten o'clock, Granny Rubin took herself off to bed. "Don't worry," she said to me. "If anything were wrong, she'd telephone."

I went into Cori's room. She had her light out, but she was awake. I told her I was sorry. I explained that Dad would get us another dog if Mom gave Cleaver away. "I don't want another dog," she cried. "I want Cleaver. And I want Dad back. I didn't even have a chance to say good-bye to Cleaver. And I'll never see him again." She began to sob some more.

I put my arm around her. We sat huddled in the blanket on the edge of her bed, looking down the driveway to the road.

A good while later a car turned in. Cori and I raced downstairs. We heard the key in the lock. The door opened and Mom came in alone. "What are you guys doing up so late?" she demanded.

"Cleaver, where's Cleaver? Where's my dog?" Cori screamed. "You gave him away, didn't you? You didn't even give me a chance to say good-bye."

Just then we heard a familiar scratch at the door and a familiar bark. "Cleaver!" Cori shouted, and pulled the door open. She grabbed Cleaver before he even got inside.

Mom looked at me. "What's the matter with her? Is she still asleep? What was she talking about?"

I shrugged my shoulders. It was too complicated to explain.

19

We sat up late while Mom told us she had gone up to Castine to see Granny Stuart, who had called to say she would like to have a good talk. Mom had taken Cleaver along to make things easier for herself, since she wasn't sure she liked Granny Stuart very much and they might need something to talk about, like their dogs.

"What did she want to talk about?" I asked.

"Your father," Mom said. "She wanted to talk about your father—her son, Edward, as she calls him—and a little bit about me and your father."

That didn't sound so encouraging. Mom didn't like people messing in her personal affairs. She even snapped at Granny Rubin when she tried to tell Mom what to do. I didn't think she would welcome any suggestions from Granny Stuart, who had pretended for a long time that Mom didn't exist.

"Did you like her?" I asked. "She was kind of nice to us." If Mom and Dad made up, I saw myself sailing a little boat around the harbor next summer.

"She was nice to me, too, in her own way. We had a good talk. She came right out and said she had no business butting into my affairs, but she thought part of what happened with your father was her responsibility. I told her no. What happened was your father's responsibility, maybe mine, too, I wasn't sure, but it wasn't hers. Dad is a grown man."

"He said he was sorry, Mom. He told us he was real sorry. He just felt trapped and he had to get out in a hurry. It was a mistake, he said, and he won't do it again. That's what he said, didn't he, Cori?"

Cori nodded agreement. She didn't usually get to take part in grown-up discussions.

"That may be, Sarah," Mom answered, "but you girls have to understand you just don't up and walk out on your family because you need more space. That's what I told his mother. I loved your father. It seemed to me we were getting along all right. He didn't say a word to me about being trapped and needing a change. He just walked out the front door of the diner one afternoon without a word—well, without more than two or three words. The next day he brought us a puppy to take his place, *this* puppy, who turned into a hundred-pound dog who eats banana ice cream every day at four o'clock."

Cleaver had his head in Mom's lap. She scratched him behind his ears.

"Granny Stuart got a puppy, too," Cori said.

"Why don't you be quiet, Cori?" I said. If she kept on with her dumb remarks, we'd never get back to Castine. "It wasn't very nice, Mom, what Dad did. We all know that. But if you still love him, maybe you should give it another try. We could move up to Maine. Granny Stuart has a lot of room."

"Ha!" Mom said. "That will be the day, when I take Ed back to his mother. If he wants space, we could move to Arizona."

I didn't think much of that. "What are you going to do, Mom?"

"I'm going to bed, that's what I'm going to do. It's a long drive to Castine and back. Let's go. Tomorrow's another day."

"I have an idea, Mom," Cori piped up again. "I think Dad left so he could give us a dog. Now that we have one, he wants to come back. What do you think?"

Mom didn't tell Cori that was the dumbest thing she ever heard of. She just laughed and said, "Maybe that's why, little Cori. Maybe that's what it was all about. Take Cleaver up to your room with you, so he won't have to sneak up those creaky steps later."

Mom didn't say any more about her visit to Granny Stuart's. The weather turned bad and we didn't make any long trips with Dad. Mostly it was supper and a movie at the mall or over in Madison, once up to Boston overnight. We went to a basketball game and the science museum.

I finished my story about the ski trip. I called it "Run-in in Stowe." Linda took it home to type up for

112

me. Mrs. Porter thought it was great. "Keep it up, Sarah," she wrote. "Writing is hard business. You have to keep at it. Give me *MORE* about your dog!" I kept my journal in the Good Luck Diner, next to the cash register, under the picture of Cleaver the watchdog.

It seemed as though winter would never end. It wasn't until late March that the ground was bare. It was the mud season, but we took Cleaver to the playing field anyway, we were so glad to be rid of the snow.

On April Fool's Day, the big blizzard struck. It turned bitter cold in the afternoon. The wind picked up, and by the time it got dark the snow was coming down so heavy you could hardly see the streetlights. Cars were creeping by like turtles in front of the diner. Mom sent Linda home early. She kept the diner open in case of an emergency outside, but no one stopped. At eight o'clock she turned out the lights and closed up. We stomped up the hill to the house. The snow was almost up to our knees.

Cleaver ran out of the house to meet us. He was all excited and danced around in the snow, snapping at the snowflakes and running around in circles, sniffing. "Let's leave him out for a while," Mom said. "He needs some exercise."

Granny Rubin said Cleaver had been carrying on all afternoon. He'd lie down under the table for a few minutes, get up and go to the door, go back under the table, and then get up again. Cori said he knew the big storm was coming because he was a snow dog. I figured Cori was probably right for once.

Cleaver didn't ask to come back in. After thirty minutes or so, I stuck my head out the door and called him. You couldn't see much, and there was no sign of Cleaver. I put on my down jacket and boots and went out to see what he was up to. There were some holes he had dug in the snow. That was all. The snow had covered up the tracks to wherever he had gone. I yelled into the wind for a while. No Cleaver.

"Let's give him another half hour," Mom said. "He must have gone out to the barn for some reason."

We yelled again in half an hour. I took a flashlight out to the barn. No sign of Cleaver. Mom said she'd wait up for a while to let Cleaver in whenever he decided to come back. She chased Cori and me off to bed.

All through the night the house rattled in the wind. When I woke up, the storm had died down a little bit, but it was still snowing. All you could see out my window was snow.

I went downstairs to find out if Mom was going to open up the diner. Mom and Dad were at the kitchen table drinking coffee. They had their boots on.

"Hi, Sarah," Dad said. He looked worried.

Mom nodded good-morning. She looked worried, too. "Cleaver didn't come in last night," she said. "I called Dad a couple of hours ago. He came over on his snowshoes. We've been out looking for the stupid dog. He has managed to get himself lost in the biggest snowstorm of the century."

"It will be all right, Nettie. Cleaver knows what to do. He's dug himself a hole in the snow somewhere and is waiting for the storm to pass. He's a mountain dog."

"He's every kind of dog but one," Mom remarked. "A good dog. That he's not."

Granny Rubin came down in her old bathrobe. When she heard that Cleaver was lost, she was more upset than any of us. "That crazy dog, not enough brains to come in out of the snow."

Cori was the last to show up. When she heard the news, she threw on her jacket over her pajamas, slipped into her boots, and ran out the door in spite of Mom's telling her to stay inside.

All of us, except Granny Rubin, spent the day looking for Cleaver. The snow finally petered out. It was up to our waists everywhere and over our heads where it had drifted. The road was a mess. Only the snowplows came by.

Just before dark, Dad and I were walking down the road toward the center of town. Mom and Cori were resting in the diner. Just before we came to the Howards' house, Dad stopped. He lifted up the flap over his red hunting hat. "Listen!" he said.

I didn't hear anything. I listened as hard as I could. Then I heard a faint whine from a big drift next to the Howards' fence. Dad forced his way into the drift. I followed. The snow was up to my chin.

The surface of the snow moved slightly in front of us. We could hear the whine better now. We started digging. First we came to Cleaver's head. He whined louder but he didn't move. We managed to get the snow off the rest of him. Still, he didn't move. Dad kneeled down to help him. Cleaver gave an awful cry.

"He's hurt," Dad said. "I think he's been hit. It looks

to me like he's hurt real bad. You stay here and watch him. I'll get help. Don't let him move, Sarah."

He went down the road to the diner. "I called the ambulance," he said when he came back with Mom and Cori. We all huddled in the drift alongside of Cleaver and tried to comfort him.

"What was he doing way down here?" Mom wondered.

"Maybe he came down to see the Howards' new dog," Cori said. "They bought a golden. Her name is Princess."

"He sure picked a bad night to go calling on his girlfriend," Mom said. "Poor old Cleaver."

"I don't know," said Dad. "I walked all the way across town in the storm to see my girlfriend. That's what love can do to you."

The ambulance showed up before Mom could answer. It came down the road, slipping and sliding, with its lights flashing. When Dad brought the two men up to where Cleaver was, they were furious.

"It's only a dog, mister. What do you think you're doing?" one of them said angrily. "We have people to look after in a storm like this. You're playing around with human lives. Come on, Harry, let's get back to the hospital."

"Wait a minute," Dad said. "Now that you're here, you might as well take the dog back with you to the animal clinic. You can't leave him here to die. That wouldn't look so good in the paper. 'Ambulance Crew Leaves Dog to Die in Snowdrift.'"

The two looked at each other. The driver shrugged. "Okay, mister, we'll drop him off at the animal clinic," the driver said. "Get the stretcher, Harry."

We eased Cleaver over onto the stretcher. He stopped whining and licked Harry's hand when he smoothed down his wet fur. Mom told Cori and me to go back to the diner. She and Dad climbed into the back of the ambulance, which went into town, red lights flashing.

Dr. Fuller put a pin in Cleaver's hip and kept him overnight. He told Mom and Dad he'd be as good as new by spring if we could keep him quiet.

Mom and Dad must have decided in the ambulance that Cleaver needed two grown-ups to look after him. Dad moved into the house that night, this time to stay, he promised.

"I guess it's all right," Mom told us. "We need another hand in the diner."

"Cleaver knew what he was doing," Granny Rubin cackled. "He figured if he caused enough trouble your mother would have to ask Ed to help out. He's not such a crazy dog after all."

Cori and I didn't say anything. We were too happy.